STO

ALLEN COUNTY PUBLIC LIBRARY

3 18

FRIEND ☑ **W9-CDW-439**

OF ACPL

A Minnetonka Summer

A
Minnetonka
Summer

E. P. DUTTON & CO., INC., NEW YORK, 1960

by BORGHILD DAHL

Illustrated by Don Lambo

Copyright, ©, 1960 by Borghild Dahl.
All rights reserved. Printed in the U.S.A.

FIRST EDITION

No part of this book may be reproduced
in any form without permission in writing
from the publisher, except by a reviewer
who wishes to quote brief passages in con-
nection with a review written for inclusion
in magazine or newspaper or broadcasts.

Library of Congress Catalog Card Number: 60-11863

CO. SCHOOLS
C500391

*To Joy Chute and her Mother
with a thank you for
their many loving kindnesses*

A Minnetonka Summer

CHAPTER ONE

SOLVEIG stood by the large kitchen table, making sandwiches filled with thick slices of cheese and cold roast pork. Her mother was over at the cupboard, packing flour and sugar and spices into a large wooden box on the floor. The morning sun streamed into the roomy kitchen, and from the shelf over the sink the cuckoo came out of its house in the clock and sang the hour of seven.

It was moving day at the Nordlands'. The family was leaving to spend the summer at Lake Minnetonka and they would not come back to their winter home in Minneapolis until school opened in the fall.

"Be sure to be generous with the sandwiches," Mrs. Nordland told Solveig. "It's going to be a long day for Sven, leading the cow out to the lake, and he will need plenty of food."

Solveig thought it would be a long, hard day for all of

them. Usually her father was able to stay home from the office and help with the moving, but today he had an important client. It wasn't going to be easy without him, especially with the new baby who was only nine months old. But her mother moved around so quickly and easily that Solveig was ashamed to voice her misgivings.

Just then Sven, the hired man, came into the kitchen. He had a red, weather-beaten face and his hands were large and gnarled. He sat down at one corner of the table and Mrs. Nordland poured some coffee for him.

"Will you be sure to let Lily have plenty of time to graze on the way?" she asked.

"Mrs. Nordland, no cow in the entire United States is going to get better treatment than I'll give Lily."

"I know," Solveig's mother said. "Only today seems to be starting out pretty hot."

"Don't forget, Mrs. Nordland, that I herded cattle up in the mountains of Norway until three years ago when I came here to be with you people. And this will be my third trip with Lily out to the lake." Then, turning to Solveig, he continued, "I'll be ready to start as soon as I finish milking her, so get on with that lunch. And don't hand out any of those fancy little things you need a microscope to see."

Solveig looked at the stack of sliced bread on the table and smiled. Sven didn't really disapprove of the way she did things. He was really very fond of her and her fifteen-year-old brother Osmund, and he put up with no end of pestering from Arnulf and Astrid, the seven-year-old twins. And as for the nine-month-old baby sister, Helga, he regarded her as nothing less than an angel.

"Well," Sven defended himself, "it's a long, hard trip from Minneapolis to the lake. A good twenty miles. And with these senseless horseless carriages around, it's getting so that a respectable man and a peaceful cow won't be safe on the streets any more." He put down his empty cup, shuffled to the door, and slammed it behind him.

"He doesn't really mean it," Solveig said. "I've heard him boasting about American inventions to some of his newly-arrived friends from Norway. Do you remember when he wouldn't touch ice cream because he said he didn't want any sleigh-riding done in his stomach, and then later we discovered him digging into the freezer?"

"Sven is a good man," said her mother. "Be careful not to hurt his feelings."

At this moment Arnulf, one of the twins, came tearing into the kitchen. He was wearing his heavy jacket and pulling Pan, the family's black-and-white hunting dog, on a leash after him.

"Where in the world do you think you're going?" Solveig asked.

"Me and Pan are all ready to walk to the lake with Sven and the cow," Arnulf replied promptly.

"You'll roast in that heavy coat," Solveig told him. "It's going to be hot today."

"Then I'll take it off and button it on Pan," Arnulf said.

"And smother him. Honestly, Mamma——"

By this time their mother had reached Arnulf's side. "Sven will have enough to do with the cow today," she said, starting to unbutton the coat. "Besides, you'd be all tired out before you reached the city limits."

Arnulf did his best to wriggle away from her. "I can ride on Pan's back."

"Pan is going to ride on top of the expressman's load," his mother told him.

Arnulf's face brightened. "Then I'll ride there too."

"You don't want to miss the ride on the streetcar and the train, do you?" his mother asked. "And what do you think Captain Deering would say if we got on his boat and you weren't with us?"

"Will he let me turn the wheel to make the steamer go?" Arnulf asked, becoming interested at once.

"I shouldn't be surprised if he did," his mother said.

How could her mother be so patient with this trying little brother of hers? Solveig wondered. Especially when she had so much to do. Yet it seemed almost no time at all before everything was piled up waiting for the expressman.

Mr. Haakonson was tall and angular, and somehow he reminded Solveig of his loose-jointed, bony horse. Long before his rickety express wagon appeared on the scene, it could be recognized by the squeaking of every screw.

Mr. Haakonson looked disapprovingly at the array of things set out ready to be loaded. "My horse isn't going to be able to pull all that," he said.

"It's almost the same amount as last year," Solveig's mother said. "And you did such a fine job of it then."

"You didn't expect me to haul this sewing machine then," Mr. Haakonson said. "Nor this cradle. And I'm sure you're bringing out more groceries this time too."

"We'll be leaving both the sewing machine and the cradle out at the lake," Solveig's mother said. "Helga won't need it after this summer, and it will come in handy when relatives or friends have little ones along."

Solveig was ashamed at the relief she felt at hearing about the cradle. There wouldn't be any more babies then, she thought. It had been a great shock to her when the twins were going on six and she learned she was to have another brother or sister. She had been too embarrassed about little Helga's coming to tell any of her friends in high school, until she had grown to love the curly-haired, blue-eyed baby so much that she couldn't refrain from talking about her. And by that time little Helga was almost six months old. But enough was enough, so it was a relief now to know that Helga was to be the last child in the family.

When Solveig was alone with her mother in the kitchen after the wagon had left, she asked, "Why do we have to hire Mr. Haakonson every year? He's nothing but an old grump and he makes you feel you have to apologize for every extra pound you put on the load."

"Mr. Haakonson is really very careful," her mother said. "In all the years he has moved us to the lake, not a single thing has been broken. He comes from the same village in Norway as your father and he needs every cent he can earn to support his large family."

There can't be many people left in Papa's village back in Norway for him to help over here in America, Solveig thought. But she refrained from saying this aloud.

Arnulf came dashing into the room. "Where are my piegons?" he called out. "I can't find my pigeons and I have to get them ready to take to the lake."

"They are already on their way, dear," his mother told him. "Sven made a nice comfortable little house for them to be in, and Mr. Haakonson found a good place for them in his wagon."

Arnulf's lower lip trembled. "But Astrid is going to take Dickie on the train in his cage," he said. He was almost in tears.

"Pigeons don't like trains and steamboats," his mother said. "Besides, their house was so big and fine we couldn't have gotten it on the streetcar."

"I'll bet Astrid's canary will be miserable in his tiny cage," Arnulf said happily as he tore out of the room.

By half past twelve the house had been straightened, lunch eaten, the dishes washed, and the family dressed and ready to start.

"We must leave early enough to allow plenty of time," Solveig's mother said. "Your father expected to be with us, so he didn't buy our tickets. Besides, in traveling with small children one can always count on emergencies."

Mrs. Nordland spoke with the assurance of one in complete control of the situation, and again Solveig marveled at her mother's calmness. The whole trip was in itself an emergency, at least until they would all be safely aboard Deering's steamer. They were going to be quite a spectacle as they walked down the street from their home to the streetcar line, her mother up ahead, carrying little Helga and Helga's special bag; Osmund, who would have charge of the hamper of lunch to be eaten on the train; clutching his hand, Astrid, one of the seven-year-old twins, holding her doll which was almost as big as herself; Solveig herself bringing up the rear, carrying the bird cage in one hand and keeping Arnulf, the other twin, in the other. And Arnulf was going to be a considerable problem, with his kite, his sailboat, a box of marbles, and three beanbags which he had kept off the load.

Everyone was out in the hall ready to leave when Astrid let out a shriek. "My doll buggy," she cried. "Mamma, you didn't put my doll buggy on the load."

"It's too late for that now, sister," Osmund said. "Come along, or you'll be left behind too."

Astrid's response was a shriek louder than the first.

Mrs. Nordland, with little Helga in her arms, went over to Astrid. "Don't cry," she said. "We'll manage somehow to take your buggy along."

"Honestly," Osmund said, "I can't manage Astrid and her doll and that big buggy too."

"Put down the bird cage for a moment, Solveig," Mrs. Nordland said, "and hold Helga." Then she relieved Arnulf of his kite and sailboat and beanbags and put them in the doll buggy. "Now, Arnulf," she said, "you can wheel the buggy. It will be much easier than keeping track of all that paraphernalia you were carrying."

Solveig gasped. Arnulf was bad enough. But Arnulf plus Astrid's doll buggy——

But her mother had relieved her of little Helga and proceeded toward the door. The children filed out, and Solveig, who had been entrusted with all the keys, carefully locked both the inside and the vestibule doors.

The sun was hot and they had to walk along the side of the street where there was no shade. Progress was slow and cumbersome. As the caravan passed Miss Bonfois' place Solveig saw her out in her rose garden. Her small hands were encased in immaculate white gloves as she snipped the lovely yellow flowers from the bushes. Solveig thought enviously that it must be wonderful to lead a life of such leisure and elegance.

There was a considerable wait for the streetcar. When one finally came, Mrs. Nordland stepped aboard first, then Astrid and Osmund. After Solveig had made sure Arnulf was in the car, she turned with her back to the steps and, holding the bird cage in one hand and clutching the doll buggy with the other, she started up herself.

"Sorry, lady, but this is no dray wagon," the conductor said. "You can't take that buggy up into the car."

Solveig tried to ignore him, but the conductor took hold of her arm. "Sorry," he said more gruffly, "if you insist on taking that buggy along, I'll have to refuse to allow you aboard."

"Conductor." It was Mrs. Nordland who spoke. "We are spending the summer at the lake. My little girl will be brokenhearted without her doll buggy."

"Isn't she rather old to be playing with dolls?" the conductor inquired.

There was a shriek from Astrid.

"It's the little girl who owns the doll buggy. Please, sir, there are only a few passengers aboard. And you'll make a little girl happy all summer."

"Oh, all right," the conductor said. "But mind you, if the car becomes crowded, I'll have to put the older girl and the buggy off."

By the time Solveig reached a seat at the far front end of the car, her cheeks burned as if they were on fire. Fortunately only a few more passengers arrived, so all the family was allowed to remain with the doll buggy until it was time to get off and take the train.

The walk to the Great Northern depot was through one of the worst districts in Minneapolis. Women with painted faces stood in doorways, and unshaven men lounged outside shabby buildings. Solveig was trying so hard to avoid the glances of both that the family had almost reached the depot when she noticed a peculiar bulge in the back of Arnulf's blouse.

"Come back here," she told him.

"What do you want?" Arnulf demanded.

"What is the matter with your back?"

"Nothing."

"Let me see."

Solveig put her hand under the waistline of Arnulf's blouse and pulled out a good-sized tin can. It had a tight cover, but from its weight Solveig realized that it was full of something.

"What is in it?" she demanded.

Arnulf made no answer.

"All right. I can't throw the can away here on the street, but I'll dispose of it in the depot if you won't tell me what you have in it."

"It's angleworms," Arnulf said sullenly.

"Of all things, why would you carry angleworms out to the lake? You know there are plenty of them out there."

"I'm going fishing right away," Arnulf said. "And I won't have time to dig worms after I get there."

"Honestly!" was all Solveig trusted herself to say.

"Are you going to throw them away?" Arnulf asked. He was almost in tears.

Another scene like the one Astrid had created at home and on the streetcar was unthinkable. "Listen," Solveig said quietly. "If you will put the can in the doll buggy and not breathe a word about the worms to Astrid, I'll let you keep them."

Fortunately, after they reached the depot, there was only time to buy the tickets and take the children to the washroom before boarding the train, so Astrid had no opportunity to inspect what was in her doll buggy. Aboard the train, Mrs. Nordland occupied a double seat with Helga, who had fallen asleep and lay curled up beside her. The others occupied another double seat. Astrid and Arnulf sat by the window, facing each other, and for a while both of them were so interested in looking out that all was quiet. Then Astrid wailed, "Arnulf is kicking me."

"I'm not."

"You are too."

"If you tell a lie on me, I'll throw angleworms at you."

This time Astrid let out a real wail. "Has Arnulf got angleworms to throw at me?" she demanded.

Solveig gave him a stern look. "Not here," she said. "And if he makes a threat like that once more, he's going to be very sorry."

Arnulf was at once completely subdued.

Mrs. Nordland, who sat across the aisle, beckoned to Solveig. "I think they are hungry," she said. "Perhaps it would be well to give them their lunch now."

"But we've been on the train only a short time. We've just left Wayzata."

"It's a considerable time since they ate at home," said her mother.

Without further protest Solveig opened the food hamper, and handed out the sandwiches. There were plenty of large, thick molasses cookies, too. Osmund munched on a cookie as he made several trips up the aisle to the water tank to fill and refill the tin cups that Solveig had remembered to take along for the twins. Afterward each of the twins had to be escorted to the toilet at the other end of the coach. Solveig felt as though everyone in the coach must be watching them.

"Solveig, can I get my box of marbles out of the doll buggy?" Arnulf asked. "I put a tablet and a pencil in there and I want to write Willie Olson a letter. I promised I'd tell him all about Lake Minnetonka."

"I promised to write Marit Bergan," Astrid said. "Have you got a pencil for me, Solveig, and some paper?"

Visions of marbles, angleworms, and goodness only

knew what cluttering the aisle of the coach gave Solveig the shivers.

"We're almost at Spring Park now," she said, "and if you aren't ready to leave when the train stops the conductor will take you on with him to Mound."

"The twins are getting tired," Mrs. Nordland said. "They were up so early—at least Arnulf was. Let them come over and sit by me for a while."

Both twins scrambled for a seat close to the window, and Mrs. Nordland made peace by sitting on the aisle herself.

As the train was drawing into the Spring Park station, the conductor came over to them. "I've set the doll buggy close to the door," he said. "I'll put it on the platform as soon as the train stops. And just sit here until I come back, madam, and I'll carry the baby for you."

Solveig heaved a sigh of relief. By this time she, too, was very tired.

Even before they reached the lake she could smell the fresh, cool air, and she drew deep breaths of it. And the smoke of Deering's steamer was deliciously different from city smoke. Captain Deering was on the dock waiting for them, and he looked exactly as he had always looked as far back as Solveig could remember—gray bushy hair and beard, a gray wool shirt turned back at the neck, baggy gray trousers, and high boots.

"Where is Mr. Nordland?" was his first greeting. "He wrote me that come what may he was going to spend more time with his family at the lake this year."

Mrs. Nordland smiled. "He was hoping to come with us until yesterday," she said. "But something came up that he had to attend to."

"Well, welcome to you all, anyway," said Captain Deering. "I'm always glad to see you city people when summer comes."

The red steamer was sending out clouds of smoke as Captain Deering took little Helga in his arms and carried her aboard. Astrid clutched her mother's hand, and Solveig kept a firm hold on Arnulf's. There was only a slight breeze on the lake. The afternoon sun was well toward the west and cast a golden light against the windows of the cottages as they passed.

Long before the steamer had reached their own settlement on the huge lake, Solveig was able to make out their home. The setting sun shone against the upstairs windows, making them look like plates of gold. The evergreens on the hillside were taller than last year, and the willow down by the boathouse drooped so low that it touched the water's edge.

What had come over her, Solveig wondered, that she should be noticing all these changes? Other years she had stood, as the twins were doing now, ready to run as soon as the rushing water at the back of the boat stopped and the steamer drew up to the dock. Even last summer she and Osmund had raced to see who would reach the front porch first.

She thought of her father and mother, standing every year on the steamer, hand in hand, and commenting on the slightest changes in their place as they approached it by water. Was she beginning to be like them now? Had she suddenly changed from a child into someone grownup? If this were true, then there were many other things that would seem different too. It was going to be interesting to find out just how she would feel and whether anything exciting was going to happen to her now that she had really become a young lady.

CHAPTER TWO

BY THE TIME the luggage was off the dock and safe on land, the twins were on the top of the hill and out of sight.

"Mamma will have enough to do carrying Helga," Solveig said to Osmund. "You had better take charge of Astrid's doll buggy, and I'll carry the bird cage and the food hamper."

Osmund frowned. "Won't I look cute trundling a doll buggy up the hill?" he said.

"Very cute. Would you rather take the bird cage?"

"No. That's just as bad."

Everything was dear and familiar to Solveig as she started up the hill from the lake shore. The strawberry patch down on the flat was a mass of bright red and green, giving promise of fresh berries for that very evening. The spot where nothing but dandelions would grow looked liked a treasure trove of gold pieces. And at the bend of the path were white daisies and dainty lacelike flowers which she and the other children called fragrant flowers or George Washington blossoms.

At the top of the hill the plum trees were covered with tiny deep-green balls which by the end of the summer would become luscious red and yellow fruit. Near them was a mighty oak that stood like a sentinel overlooking the lake front, and Solveig stopped for an instant to gaze at it. Once she had climbed that oak, and after she had reached its top branches she had looked down and seen the water far beneath her. She had suddenly become so dizzy and scared that she had almost lost her hold on the branch, and her heart had been in her mouth until, after what had seemed an eternity, she had managed to climb down and was safe on the ground once more.

"The first thing Sven does tomorrow," Solveig's mother said, "is to cut the grass with a scythe. It is far too long to use the lawn mower. And we'll dry it out well, for it will make a soft filling for the mattress bags to use as beds on the floor when we have an overflow of company."

Solveig came to with a start. Company. Yes, there was sure to be plenty of it this year as always. And company meant extra work from dawn to dark.

The twins were back again, each holding a white peony. "There are lots more," Astrid called out. "Red ones too. And all the other flowers are in bloom. Can we pick them all?"

Solveig opened her mouth to scold the twins, but her mother had already begun to speak. "The peonies you have already picked for me are so large and beautiful that each one will make a bouquet by itself. So let us save the other flowers until later."

The children thrust their flowers into their mother's

hand and were off. All the rest of the way up to the house they turned somersaults through the deep grass.

Inside the house, Mrs. Nordland said, "The first thing to do will be to get into different clothes. I see that Astrid already has grass stains on her white dress and there are some on Arnulf's blouse. Fortunately I'll be able to remove them with lemon and salt."

She put little Helga into Solveig's arms while she went upstairs to find some old clothes and returned with her arms full. She helped Astrid into a faded blue gingham, and Astrid started to giggle.

"It comes way above my knees, Mamma," she said. "And look at the sleeves. They are almost up to my elbows."

"You have grown, child. Tomorrow I'll cut off the sleeves, and then this dress will make a fine bathing suit for you this summer."

Osmund had shot up so much during the past winter that he was unable to get into anything he had worn the previous summer, but a discarded pair of his father's overalls, though slightly baggy at the waist, would do for now. Solveig put on a green and white plaid gingham and her mother a lavender percale.

"Now, Solveig, I think you and Osmund had better get the windmill started," Mrs. Nordland said.

"Can we go along?" Arnulf begged.

"Who was it that promised to look after Helga?" Solveig reminded him.

"Aw, shucks," Arnulf protested. But he went out on the back porch where Astrid had already stationed herself beside the baby.

As she was walking toward the windmill, Solveig stopped suddenly. "Look," she said, pointing to the wheel. "The swallows are back and sitting all around it up there. I just don't like to disturb them."

"Then don't," Osmund said cheerfully. "Only count yourself a committee of one to carry all the water up from the lake to water the lawns and grounds, to wash the family clothes, scrub the floor, and——"

Solveig took hold of his arm. "That's enough," she said. "But you might at least show a slight interest in those lovely swallows that come back year after year."

"I'm interested in them all right," Osmund told her. "But I'm even more interested in a family of human beings that also comes back year after year."

It was hard work pulling the huge hasp from its hook, and it took the combined strength of both of them to accomplish it. But as soon as the steel wire that held the wheel hung loosely down below, a blast of wind came. At once the wheel began to turn and the pump on the wooden platform began to draw water from the lake. And, with one accord, the swallows took flight.

"Poor things," Solveig said sorrowfully. "I wonder where they will be able to perch now?"

"If it's any comfort to you, just look over to the play-house roof," Osmund said. "There's a bunch of them sitting on the peak of it already."

The water in the kettles on the stove was just warm enough for mopping up the porches and the floors in the house when Edith Sather came over from next door. She had brought a pitcher of milk, and in her basket were eggs, a pat of butter, a loaf of bread, and a plate of cold meat. "We heard you arrive," she said. "So Mamma sent me up with a few things to tide you over until your load gets here."

She looked just the same as always, her sandy hair

streaked with gray and her black-and-white calico dress neat and clean. She was so much a part of every summer at the lake that until now Solveig had taken her for granted. But now, as she stood on the porch with the basket hung over her arm, Solveig felt sudden warmth and gratitude for all her kindness.

"Your mother is a good neighbor," Mrs. Nordland said gratefully. "Tell her many, many thanks."

After Edith Sather had left, Solveig said, "Mamma, I think the strawberries are ripe enough to eat. They looked red as we walked up the hill."

"It would certainly be nice to have some for supper tonight and for breakfast in the morning," Mrs. Nordland said. "Only it's hard to take the time to pick them."

"If Osmund and I went down to the patch, we could make quick work of it," Solveig said.

The twins came running into the kitchen. "We want to go along," they begged.

Mrs. Nordland said sternly, in a tone of voice she seldom used, "If you ever leave little Helga alone again when you are supposed to be minding her, you will both be severely punished."

The strawberries were certainly ripe. In no time Solveig and Osmund had picked a heaping dishpan full. "And you couldn't see we had picked any," Solveig reported, "there are such a lot of them down there."

"That means we'll have to get at some canning tomorrow," Mrs. Nordland said.

The porches and all the floors had been washed, supper had been eaten, and little Helga and the twins had been put to bed when Mr. Haakonson, the expressman, arrived with the load. The wagon had not come to a stop when Pan, the hunting dog, let out a yelp and tried fiercely to get free from the rope that tied him to the seat. Mrs. Nordland and Solveig and Osmund had been watching for the load and were out in the yard as soon as the wagon turned in from the main road. An instant later Arnulf, in his nightshirt, came tearing out the back door.

"Can Pan sleep with me?" he called out, running over to the wagon and beginning to tug at the rope. The dog licked Arnulf's face, put his front paws around his neck, and kept letting out yips of joy.

"Take the dog and the boy away," the expressman said crossly, "so I can start to unload."

"But it's late," Mrs. Nordland protested. "Won't you come in and eat some supper and rest until tomorrow morning? It will be time enough to unload then."

"I'm a poor workingman," the expressman growled. "So I can't lie around the lake lazily like rich folks."

"But you need to eat and rest and so will the horse," said Mrs. Nordland.

"I have eaten. I brought food from home for myself and the horse. And I'll sleep in the wagon if you'll only let me get started."

"Accommodate the gentleman and you'll accommodate the family," Osmund said in a loud voice. "The sooner we part, the better."

His mother cast him a reproving look, but it was lost on Osmund for he had started for the wagon. In a little while he was back on the porch, staggering under the heavy weight of the boxes, the barrels, and the old sewing machine, which was clumsy to carry because of the handle that was needed to make it work.

Osmund certainly is growing up, Solveig thought as she worked with him. He was stretching out to become tall and slender like their father, and yet with his brown eyes and hair he resembled their mother more and more. It was queer how girls, before they were grown up, never paid any attention to how a younger brother looked.

"Would you like me to pay you now?" Mrs. Nordland asked the expressman.

"No," he said gruffly. "I'll settle with your husband, the architect. It's been so hard on me and the horse today that I'll have to charge more than we bargained for."

Inside the house Solveig said, "I'm going to tell Papa that if he insists on hiring that man next year, he ought at least to make him carry the things indoors. He makes it unpleasant for everybody."

"He did look tired," Mrs. Nordland said.

"Who isn't?" Solveig demanded.

After Osmund had gone to bed, Solveig and her mother went on unpacking by the light of the lantern, which had to be carried from room to room because there was no oil in any of the lamps. The old clock in the parlor struck twelve.

"I'm worried about Sven and the cow," Mrs. Nordland said. "I wonder if something could have happened to them. I don't see how they could have gotten lost. Sven has made the trip several times and always found his way before."

"Why don't you go to bed, Mamma? I'll sit up for Sven."

"I am a little tired," her mother conceded. "But you are too."

"Not if I just sit up and read."

"Well, all right. But don't stay up much longer. Sven may have decided to stay overnight with someone along the way."

Solveig carried the lantern out on the front porch.

But it was so peaceful and beautiful out there that she blew out the light and sat down in the hammock. The moon had come up and cast its reflection in a shirred ribbon across the great lake. On both sides of the grounds the white trunks of the birch trees stood out like ghosts with shawls of leaves over their heads. There was a constant undertone of the chirping of insects and every once in a while the call of some bird or animal that was also keeping a night vigil. The white picket fence above the terrace played at hide-and-seek as the towering branches of oaks and lindens were tossed about by spasmodic gusts of wind.

Of course she hoped that no ill had befallen Sven and the cow. But their absence gave her the excuse to sit here in peace and quiet, something her mother would have objected to under ordinary circumstances. With so many younger children in the family there was always confusion and commotion. Her mother did not seem to notice it, or if she did, she didn't seem to mind. Mothers must be blessed with more patience and better nerves than older sisters.

Solveig was still going over family problems in her mind when she heard a long-drawn-out moo. She jumped from the hammock, rushed out the screen door of the front porch, and ran around the house to the back. Slowly coming up the main road was Sven, plodding along and leading the family cow.

In no time Solveig was beside him. "Everyone else is in bed," she said in a low voice. "Has Lily been fed and watered and milked?"

"Yes," said Sven wearily.

"All right. Take her to the barn and tie her up for the rest of the night, and then I'll give you something to eat."

Sven sank into the kitchen chair while Solveig set out the food for him—a bowlful of strawberries with some of the milk Edith Sather had brought, cold meat sandwiches, and hot coffee which she managed to prepare by stirring up the embers still alive in the kitchen stove.

"Did you get lost?" Solveig asked finally.

"Of course not. But it's a big walk and the day has been hot. The trip wasn't an easy one for either Lily or me, and I couldn't see that there was any hurry."

"We could have used some of the milk for supper," Solveig said. "By the way, when did you milk her?"

Sven looked sheepish. "Well, I was sitting by the side of the road and some cats came along, and they looked hungry, and so I fed them in the only way I could." For the first time since his arrival there was a smile on Sven's face.

"Mamma and Papa are going to be very grateful to you for taking such good care of Lily," Solveig said, picking up the empty dishes.

Sven got up from his chair. "Tell your mother to wake me if I oversleep," he said. "It was a little early when I fed the cats Lily's milk, and she shouldn't wait too long to be milked tomorrow."

Left alone downstairs, Solveig was in no mood to go to bed. The night was far too beautiful. Besides, this was her one chance for goodness knew how long to get at the thrilling book Selma Lofgren had let her borrow just before school closed. She had read only snatches of it so far after she was in bed at night. Coming out to the lake, she had carried it safely in the food hamper without anyone knowing. Now she was in the most exciting part of the entire story.

She picked up the lantern and went to the table in the parlor and to the little drawer where she had hidden the book. She took it out and by the light of the lantern read its title for the hundredth time: *Only the Governess,* by Marie Corelli.

She went out on the porch, since moonlight would be a perfect setting for the part of the story she had come to. Would the handsome grown-up son of the family propose marriage to Miss Rossiter, the governess who had come to tutor the smaller children? And would the rich, aristocratic family accept her if he did?

In no time Solveig was lost to everything in the world except the romance that she was enjoying with the two lovers. It was only when she reached the last page and knew they were looking forward to a life of uninterrupted bliss that she looked up and realized the dawn was breaking.

She tiptoed up to her room and put the book under her pillow. Tomorrow she would lock it in the drawer, which was her one chance for privacy against the curiosity of the twins. The book would stay there until fall when she went back to the city and could return it to Selma Lofgren. It was certainly generous of Selma to let her keep it all summer. On further thought, she might even read the book once more. It was such a very beautiful love story.

CHAPTER THREE

SEVERAL days later Solveig woke up with the feeling that something very pleasant was about to happen. Then she remembered. It was Sunday morning, and her father had arrived from the city the night before. He had looked very imposing in his light-gray suit and his blue tie with the beautiful gold horseshoe stickpin. In one hand he had carried his white Panama hat and in the other the evening paper and the covered basket in which he always brought fresh meat and other provisions, and Solveig would always remember the tender smile on his face when he stooped to kiss her mother.

Still only half awake, she heard her father call from downstairs, "Everyone get dressed and ready for the flag raising."

Always on Sunday morning at the lake, the day was started by raising the flag that stood at the top of the terrace overlooking the water. In bright sunshine the gilt ball at the top of the flagpole could be seen by people far out on the lake, and when the flag showed its full size on Sunday in a stiff breeze it was visible as far away as Fagerness.

Raising the flag on Sunday morning was a custom Mr. Nordland had brought with him from Norway. He often told how, on the Lord's Day, you could go into any village and be greeted by the Norwegian flag everywhere, even before the home of the humblest cottager.

Solveig could hear the twins racing to see who could dress the fastest, and there was considerable activity in Osmund's room. She put on her own clothes as quickly as she could.

When she reached the kitchen, her mother had already built a brisk fire and the kettle was sending forth steam from its spout. "I thought I would get breakfast started," she said. "Everyone will be hungry when we come back from raising the flag."

On her way to the cupboard to get the dishes Solveig stopped to kiss Helga, who was sitting in her high chair. "That's for you, little early bird," she said, and Helga responded with a friendly gurgle.

There was a sound of footsteps on the stairs and the next moment her father appeared in the doorway, a twin clinging to each arm. "Is everyone ready for the flag raising?" he asked. Osmund came after him with their huge American flag over one arm. Solveig took Helga out of her high chair, and the family all started for the flagpole.

The flag was always raised with the greatest formality. First the family formed a semicircle around the pole. Then Osmund handed the flag to his father. Slowly Mr.

Nordland unfolded it while Osmund, standing close by, held one end, being careful that not even the tip of the flag touched the ground. Then Mr. Nordland tied the rope of the flag into tight knots, fastening the flag to the rope of the pole, and slowly the flag was hoisted. After it had reached the top and had blown out to its full size, Mr. Nordland gave the signal for all to place their hands on their hearts. Solveig put little Helga's hand on her heart and she, seeing what the others were doing, kept it there. Then all, in unison, repeated the pledge to the flag.

When the ceremony was over, Mr. Nordland said, as he always did at this moment, "Thank God every day, children, that you are Americans. You have a rich Norwegian heritage, but you live in the most wonderful land in all the world." He spoke so earnestly that even though Solveig had heard the same words many times she felt, as she always did, a sensation akin to awe.

Since there was the addition of Helga this summer, it took some rearranging to get the whole family seated at the breakfast table on the porch. Mr. Nordland sat at the head of the table, and when an attempt was made to place Helga in her high chair at the opposite end she burst into loud wails, so she was put close to her father on the right side of the table. Solveig sat next, and Astrid's place was beside her mother. Arnulf sat at his father's left, then came Osmund, and Sven was at Mrs. Nordland's right.

"Can't Papa wait to read from the Bible until we've eaten?" Arnulf begged. "I'm hungry."

Without answering him, his mother made a sign to her husband and he began to read. It was the passage about how Jesus calmed the storm and walked upon the water.

"I'll bet it was winter so He walked on ice," Astrid said.

"How clever of you," Osmund said witheringly. "Waves of ice must have been most spectacular."

"Children," was all Mr. Nordland said. But the discussion of the miracle ceased abruptly.

It seemed to Solveig that Sunday-morning breakfast at the lake was always the most enjoyable meal of the week. There was the setting of the screened porch with the lake close by, the fragrance of evergreens and flowers, the presence of her father who was at home so seldom during the summer. And the food itself.

No one could make buns as good as those her mother made. The children called them pocketbook buns, because she pushed them so close together in the pan that they came out thin and very high. Then there was her delicious rye bread and sweet butter and jam, and the best-smelling coffee in the world for the grownups. But best of all was the fish, which her mother alone could prepare properly. Only fresh sunfish or crappies would do, and these were skinned and deboned except for the one large bone down the back. The fish were browned in butter, and just before it was ready to be taken out of the pan her mother poured cream over it.

After breakfast was over Mrs. Nordland said, "Now, Solveig, you go upstairs and get ready for church. You've had a busy week and it will do you good to get out."

"But, Mamma, the dishes and——"

"Sven will help me with the dishes. He has offered to freeze the ice cream too. Osmund is going to row over to the station for the Sunday paper. Your father will take the twins while he waters his apple trees. You know how he enjoys that. And little Helga is already sleepy and will be having her nap."

"I don't especially care to attend church," Solveig protested. "Why can't I go to the station with Osmund instead?"

"It is very kind of Reverend Sandness to invite us lake people to his cottage every Sunday for services. I feel the least we can do is to have the family represented."

"Oh, all right," said Solveig, but she went upstairs to change her clothes in anything but a devout mood. Her father was very strict about all the children studying their catechism and Bible history and committing to memory passages from the Bible, but he himself very seldom attended church. And when Solveig went alone—especially on the porch of Reverend Sandness's cottage, where everyone could be observed—she felt ill at ease. So many families of Norwegian heritage came in a body, from the babe in arms to the grandparents, that Solveig somehow felt she ought to apologize for her own family.

At the Sandness cottage the seats for the congregation were set along both sides of the screened porch, and a table at one end was covered with a white doily on which had been placed a vase of petunias and a Bible. There was no instrument to accompany the singing, which started off pitch, although Solveig did her best to follow along with the others. The sermon was in Norwegian and seemed to have something to do with unleavened bread, but Solveig realized she would be able to give only a poor account of it should her mother question her.

At the end of the services Solveig was about to make her escape when Mrs. Overgaard stopped her. "I suppose your parents are too busy to attend church," she told Solveig. "Be sure to greet them from me."

"Papa came on the late train last night and has to take the seven o'clock tomorrow morning. And it isn't easy for Mamma to leave Helga." Then, before Mrs. Overgaard could say anything else, Solveig managed to get away.

All the way home she smarted under the implied reproof against her parents. She would have liked to remind Mrs. Overgaard of the time her husband was so drunk he fell off the dock and into the lake, but of course she couldn't. Her mother would have been ashamed and hurt if she had forgotten her good behavior.

The kitchen was fragrant with boiling coffee when Solveig reached home. There was a huge platter piled high with cinnamon rolls standing on the kitchen table, and her mother was taking a pitcher of milk out of the icebox. "We're having our forenoon snack in the grape arbor," she said. "Put on your blue gingham dress and come out there."

It was shady and pleasant out in the grape arbor. The vines were loaded with clusters of green grapes and the large leaves were fresh and shiny from the frequent rains. Mrs. Nordland had spread a white cloth over the table, and there were cups and saucers and glasses at all the places.

"Come and sit by me," her father called out. "I haven't seen much of my oldest daughter since I came out here."

As Solveig sat down he patted her shoulder and she felt her face glow with pleasure. She loved her father almost more than her mother and she admired him as she did no other person in the world, even though in many ways his views on life differed from most of the other fathers she knew.

"Were there many people in church?" Solveig's mother asked.

"The porch was full," Solveig said.

"I could eat a barrel of cinnamon rolls," Arnulf said, his mouth full as he spoke.

"Don't try to chew and talk at the same time," Osmund told him.

"Did you get the paper?" Solveig asked.

"He's already read the funnies to us," Astrid said.

"When I get big I'm going to get up early and row over to the station and buy a whole bunch of papers and go around the lake and sell them for lots more than I pay for them and get rich," Arnulf said between bites.

"I'm going along and get rich too," Astrid said.

"Copycat."

"Such twinly devotion," said Osmund.

The bickering of the twins annoyed Solveig a little, but as she looked around the table she couldn't help a feeling of pride and tenderness for her younger brothers and sisters: little Helga in a white dress trimmed with beading and with a blue ribbon drawn through it; Astrid in pink with a crisp pink bow in her short hair; Arnulf and Osmund in snowy white shirts like their father's. If only her mother weren't so easy with them and would keep them more under control. Then Solveig was ashamed of herself for even thinking something of a critical nature about her sweet, loving mother.

"Markus, were you and the children going to play croquet?" her mother asked.

Arnulf and Astrid shot out of their seats. "Papa is going to be my partner," Astrid called as she raced out of the grape arbor.

"Who cares?" Arnulf shouted after her. "Osmund and I could beat you if we played left-handed."

"Can you take care of Helga while you play croquet?" Mrs. Nordland asked.

"I'll watch Helga," Sven said. "I haven't anything else to do."

"You are always so helpful," Mrs. Nordland said gratefully.

She and Solveig went into the kitchen, which seemed very hot after the coolness of the grape arbor.

"I've baked a couple of strawberry pies," said Mrs. Nordland, "because your father likes them so much. The beef roast is already in the oven, and we can sit on the porch while we prepare the vegetables."

There were potatoes and carrots and whole onions to be placed around the roast in the large pan. And lettuce from the garden. The family liked leaf lettuce best, with the vinegar and sugar sprinkled over it. And there were radishes also from the garden, and watermelon pickles from last year's canning.

"We'll eat a little before three o'clock," Mrs. Nordland said. "That will give plenty of time to let the food settle before your father takes you children bathing down in the lake."

All the children looked forward to the swimming party in the late afternoon every Sunday. Their father was an excellent swimmer and he had taught each of the children as soon as their mother had permitted them to go into the lake. As usual, their mother had made over old clothes into bathing suits for all of them. The girls' were of heavy dark-blue duck cloth. The boys' were old overalls cut down to fit them. Only their father had a regular bathing suit bought in a store.

Solveig loved to swim, and in other years she had been able to outdistance Osmund easily. But this year he was all over his splashing, which had wasted his strength, and he showed great speed. Solveig was just able to reach the dock ahead of him, but it was nip and tuck.

Their father kept close to the shore and spent all his time in the water helping Astrid and Arnulf to learn to swim. Solveig marveled at his patience, for she knew that her father was himself a very good swimmer. He had taught both her and Osmund many years ago. Did people develop patience by becoming parents? she wondered.

Up at the house again, the bathers found a large pitcher of lemonade and one of grape juice waiting for them on the porch table. There was a platter of her mother's thick cream cookies and another of her large molasses cookies. In no time everything was eaten.

"If anyone gets hungry after this," Mrs. Nordland said, "I'll make some sandwiches."

Little Helga fell asleep immediately after her evening bath, and when Astrid and Arnulf were told it was their bedtime they were so tired that they made no objections to going upstairs by themselves. Mrs. Nordland went up later to hear their prayers and came down almost immediately to say that both children were already asleep.

Osmund was deep in a book and lost to everything around him. For a moment Solveig waited for her father to begin a discussion about something she would be interested in or suggest a game of dominoes or checkers as he sometimes did in the evening when everything had quieted down. Instead, he and her mother began talking over some business about which she understood little and cared less.

She went out to the porch and sat down. There was still moonlight, as there had been all week, and she opened the screen door and went to the top of the hill. She could hear laughter and talking that came from the water in front of the cottages down below toward the west. The people there seemed to enjoy themselves, day and night, every day of the week. Work, it seemed, was not a part of their lives, at least not while they were at the lake.

As far as Solveig was able to see, the only clothes that ever hung on their lines to dry were wet bathing suits, and the weeds around the cottages were never cut. Yet it would be nice, just for a change, to have absolutely nothing to do as they did and to concentrate on having rollicking fun.

CHAPTER FOUR

"Mamma, we've been out here nearly two weeks, and except for the Sathers and the butter-and-egg people, we've seen nobody. We might as well be stranded on a desert island."

Solveig helped herself to a generous spoonful of strawberry jam and spread it over her rye bread. She and the children and her mother were having breakfast on the back porch.

"Is it as bad as that?" her mother asked, smiling.

"I haven't even been over to the hotel to ask for mail," said Solveig.

Osmund looked up from his dish of cereal. "She thinks she has a packet of heart-throb letters waiting for her over there," he said. "As for me, I bade a fond farewell to all my loving friends before leaving the city and we'll have a reunion in the fall. As for all my dear relatives, close and distant, they will probably all be out here to pay us their respects before the summer is over."

"Osmund," Mrs. Nordland said sternly, "you musn't say such things. Arnulf hangs on everything you say, and such expressions don't sound well coming from either of you."

"Oh, all right," Osmund said.

"Mamma," said Solveig, "couldn't Osmund and I row over to the station this morning and see if there is any mail for us at the hotel?"

Mrs. Nordland hesitated. "I had intended to cut out a dress for Astrid this morning, and that would mean leaving the housekeeping to you. But it won't matter too much if I start the dress tomorrow."

"I want to go to the station too," Astrid said.

"No tag tails, please," said Osmund.

"We'll buy a box of cracker jack for you and one for Arnulf," Solveig promised.

When they were down at the lake shore, Solveig asked if they were going to use both pairs of oars.

"No," Osmund said. "The sky is overcast and it looks like good fishing weather. I thought one of us could troll on the way back. We ought to catch something if we row near the shore."

Solveig enjoyed sitting in the back seat, feeling the soft south breeze against her face. Osmund was a good rower, and even with one pair of oars they made rapid progress.

When they reached a point directly between Fagerness and Deering's Island, Solveig said, "Do you want me to row now?"

"Sit where you are. No changing of seats out on the lake. That's one law that Papa laid down to me when I was younger than Arnulf is now, and I've always obeyed it."

After they had reached shore, pulled their boat well up on the beach, and put out their anchor, Captain Deering leaned over the side of his steamer to call to them. "There's a letter for you people up at the hotel. I told the clerk I knew you and that I'd deliver it if it wasn't called for today."

"There, you see," Solveig told Osmund as they walked up the path to the hotel.

She always got a thrill out of the sight of the beautiful Hotel Del Otero, and this morning it appeared even more imposing than usual. Flowers of every shape and color were in bloom along the fence and on both sides of the walk that led from the gate to the screened porch. Fashionably dressed grownups and children with Negro nurses strolled on the green velvety lawn. Other people, wearing beautiful clothes, were sitting on the porch and in the hotel lobby. Solveig felt self-conscious in her blue-and-white gingham dress, and her cheeks burned with embarrassment as she looked at Osmund's well-worn overalls and his bare feet.

"You should have worn shoes and stockings," she murmured.

"What for?" Osmund demanded.

They had almost reached the clerk's desk when a girl about Osmund's age and a boy who was somewhat older came into the hotel lobby. Both of them were dressed in white and carrying tennis racquets.

"I'd love to learn to play tennis," said Solveig in a low voice.

"I'd rather bowl if I had the price of a game," said Osmund. "That reminds me, didn't you promise to buy the kids some cracker jack? I'll run down to the casino and buy it while you get the mail."

Solveig untied her handkerchief and gave him the two nickels she had brought along.

When she asked the clerk if there was any mail for the Nordlands on Saga Hill, his face brightened.

"There has been a letter here for some time. I was on the point of returning it to the sender when Captain Deering said he would deliver it to you if it wasn't claimed today."

The clerk handed Solveig a letter. It was addressed to her mother and the postmark said Decorah, Iowa. As she walked out of the hotel lobby and down the boardwalk. she tried to think whom her mother knew living there. She had almost reached the end of the path leading down to the lake when she remembered that an old nurse who cared for her and Osmund years ago had gone there to live. But, as far as Solveig knew, her mother had not heard from her in a long time.

Solveig stood by the boat waiting for Osmund to appear. What could have happened to him? If they intended to row along the shore and troll they would be late getting home.

At last he came running, all out of breath.

"Where in the world have you been so long?" Solveig demanded.

"You remember the girl and the fellow in the lobby with the tennis racquets? Well, I'd bought the cracker jack and was rushing out of the pavilion when I bumped right into the girl and almost knocked her down."

"I hope you excused yourself," Solveig said.

"I couldn't. We were both laughing so hard. And then they introduced themselves. The girl's name is Patricia Worthington and her brother's name is Morton. They're from St. Louis and are spending the summer at the hotel. And they'd like to meet you some time."

"Osmund, you know very well they only said that to be polite. Why would they want to meet us when they have the chance to be with all those elegant people in the hotel?"

"I'll bet they get good and tired of such a big dose of elegance. I know I would."

"Osmund, how can you talk like that?"

"Because you're so silly to be impressed by stiff high collars and swishing skirts." As he spoke Osmund pulled up the anchor and put it in the front of the boat.

"I'll row," Solveig said. "I don't like to pull in the fish and take them off the hook."

After they had gotten under way, Osmund asked, "Did you get the letter?"

"Yes. I think it's from Jordine. You remember she used to be with us years ago."

"Do you suppose she plans to pay us a visit?" Osmund asked.

"If she does, she'll at least be giving us a warning."

"I'll put up a tent for her down by the boathouse," said Osmund, "and she can fend for herself."

"Osmund, don't you dare talk like that. If Arnulf heard you, he'd be likely to quote you in front of somebody and Mamma would be so ashamed she'd never get over it."

On further thought, Solveig decided there might be something important in the letter. Since it had been held so long at the hotel, they had better let the trolling go and row straight across the lake, the shortest way home.

When they had landed on their own beach Solveig said, "I'll leave you to pull up the boat and put out the anchor,

Osmund. It won't take you nearly as much time as I wasted, waiting for you while you were cultivating the acquaintance of the Worthingtons."

In the kitchen her mother was taking a large pan of corn bread out of the oven, and Solveig said at once, "Mamma, Osmund wants us to start going around with some of those fine people staying at the hotel, and I think we shouldn't. Don't you agree with me?"

Mrs. Nordland set the pan of corn bread on the kitchen table. "I don't understand. Surely Osmund hasn't forced himself on any of the guests there."

At that moment Osmund came into the kitchen. "What's Solveig trying to tell you?" he demanded.

"I simply said you wanted us to start going around with——"

"How silly can you be? All I said was that after I had bumped into Patricia Worthington at the pavilion, she and her brother Morton and I got started talking for a little while. And before they left, they said they would like to meet Solveig."

"It was more than a little while. I'll bet I stood half an hour waiting for you."

"It's wonderful how a few minutes can expand into a full half hour in your reckoning," Osmund mocked.

"Anyway, Mamma, when Osmund came back finally, he——"

"All I said was that Patricia and her brother said they'd like to meet her."

"They were only being polite, Mamma."

"What makes you think they didn't mean what they said?" her mother asked gently.

"Because she writes off all people who stay at hotels as liars," Osmund said.

"They're rich, and we're only lake cottagers." Solveig was growing more and more petulant as the argument continued.

"It's a cinch," Osmund remarked, "that I'd rather be a lake cottager than one of those hotel guests sitting around sweating in high stiff collars and heavy coats."

His mother burst into hearty laughter. "You are certainly fortunate to be saved from such a terrible fate," she said. Then she grew serious. "Doesn't it occur to you, Solveig, that these young people may be looking for something other than mere wealth in selecting their friends?"

"There, you see," said Osmund triumphantly. "Furthermore, neither Patricia nor her brother asked me one single thing about my father's bank account, and they didn't volunteer how many millions their father had stashed away either."

"Next time you two go to the hotel for mail and happen to meet these young people, you can certainly be cordial to them. It will be easy to find out whether they wish to continue the acquaintance. After all, I see no reason for your being any more impressed with them than they would be with you."

Osmund cast Solveig a triumphant look. Then he asked, "Did you give Mamma her letter?"

"Oh, I forgot." Solveig took it out of the deep pocket of her gingham skirt. "I think it's from Jordine."

"The letter will have to wait," said her mother, "until we get dinner out of the way. The twins are too hungry to postpone it any longer."

After the meal was over and the dishes washed and dried, Solveig asked her mother, "Shall I get the letter for you now?"

"I am just going to finish sweeping the kitchen floor,"

said her mother, "and then I will rest a little in the hammock on the front porch. I've been on my feet much of the morning, and it will be good to sit."

Solveig had put the letter on the clock shelf in the parlor so that it would not be lost, and her mother was settled comfortably in the hammock when she returned with it in her hand.

"Read it aloud to me, dear," her mother said. "I left my glasses upstairs. I used them for reading the lesson of the day in my book of devotions last night after I went to bed, and I forgot to take them down with me this morning."

"The letter is in English, but Jordine writes that peculiar Norwegian script I can't read very well. But I'll do my best to make it out."

"Thank you, dear," her mother said as she settled back to listen.

CHAPTER FIVE

SOLVEIG started to read the letter from Jordine to her mother. It began:

"Dear Mrs. Nordland,

I have long meant to write you and thank you for the beautiful pillowcases you sent. You must have thought either that I did not receive them or that I did not appreciate your wonderful present.

The reason I haven't written is that we have had sickness here all winter and even now the baby is far from well. The two older children, our son Ragnar and our daughter Milda, got the whooping cough before Christmas and just after New Year the baby took it too. There were weeks when I hardly dared go to sleep at night for fear of one or the other getting a coughing spell and choking.

The spring has been so cold and damp here around Decorah that I have not been able to put in my vegetable garden.

But perhaps it is just as well because I have been having a little trouble with my back and I sometimes have a hard time bending over or getting upstairs to the bedroom.

Haying is just over and we are blessed with a very good crop this year, except that it was difficult to dry and had to be salted before it was put into the haymow. It means so much for the winter to have a good crop of hay.

Harvest will not begin for several weeks and we are hoping that the weather will clear and the crops will be good. And it would be nice if the children could have some sunshine during this breathing spell. During harvest and threshing everyone but the baby has to pitch in and help from early morning until bedtime.

It is pouring again today, but, thanks be, Lars has inside work to do. He and the children are repairing harnesses in the kitchen and keeping an eye on the baby while I write this letter. If the roads are dry enough tomorrow he will take the cream to the creamery and then he has promised to post this letter. But if it keeps on being too wet, you will understand why it will seem so long to reach you.

As I read over this letter, it seems as though I have been complaining and I did not mean to at all. I only wanted you to know why I had failed to write and thank you. And I hear the baby crying now, so that I cannot write the letter over again.

Again I thank you. Please greet your fine children and your husband. And to you, my dear friend, I send my most sincere affection.

Your devoted former hired girl and always friend,

Jordine."

For a while after Solveig had finished reading the letter they both sat silent. Then her mother said, "Poor Jordine. In spite of her courage and her devotion to her family, she sounds both tired and a little discouraged."

"It's a hard life on a farm," Solveig said.

Again her mother was silent for a while. Suddenly she said, "Solveig, I am going to write a letter this very evening and invite Jordine and the children to come and visit us during the lull between the haying and the harvest."

Solveig sat as if stunned. "Mamma, you can't mean that."

"Why not? During the summer we can always bed any number of people out here."

"But—but with our family there would be two babies to be carried around, and no doubt the older children would be of an age to have fights with the twins, and——"

"I am sure Jordine's children would be well behaved."

"Mamma," Solveig persisted, "June is the month those distant relatives of Papa's usually descend upon us. Not to mention people from town who come uninvited to surprise us for a day or longer."

Her mother smiled. "You make it sound very tragic, dear. With only a very few exceptions we really enjoy our guests out here."

"But, Mamma, it would be nice to have a few days by ourselves here once in a while."

"We shall. Remember the summer has just begun. And weren't you the one who complained about being stranded on a desert island?"

"Anyway," said Solveig, "if we have to have company, why can't we ask people it would be fun to have?"

"What makes you think we wouldn't have fun while Jordine is here?"

"She certainly doesn't sound exciting, and neither do those three farm children."

"Solveig, when Jordine lived with us, she cared for you and Osmund as lovingly as if you had been her own children. After Osmund was born she relieved me so completely of all responsibility that I was able to rest and finally get my strength back."

"But Papa paid her, didn't he?" Solveig demanded.

"Of course she received wages, and for that time rather generous ones. But there are certain things in life, Solveig, that are too precious to be paid for in money. Jordine's kindness to me and to you and to Osmund, too, comes under that category."

"If she only wasn't so—sort of different, Mamma," Solveig said weakly.

"Jordine came from Norway as a poor immigrant. She had worked hard over here. To me, her loving heart makes up for any eccentricities you may object to about her."

Jordine accepted the invitation by return mail, with unmistakable gratitude and joy, and Solveig tried to tell herself that she was pleased the family was coming. But it was one thing to give charity to people, or to pay them good wages, and quite another to welcome them into your own home. She tried not to think these thoughts, knowing that her mother would have disapproved of them, but telling herself they were wrong did not seem to make any difference.

The morning that Jordine was to arrive with the children Solveig and Osmund set out in the rowboat to meet the ten-o'clock train.

"There will be a good many in the boat," Mrs. Nordland said, "but I do not want Jordine to go to the expense of taking the steamer. You, Osmund, had better do the rowing on the way back. Ask Jordine to sit in the back seat with the baby. You, Solveig, keep Milda with you on the widest rower's seat. And it will be all right for Ragnar to be in the little front seat. Only caution everyone to sit absolutely still in the boat and on no account to stand up."

Solveig offered to do the rowing going over, and Osmund made no objection. They arrived a short time before the train was scheduled to come in and sat down in the front row of seats out on the station platform.

"Why don't you go up to the hotel and see if there is any mail?" Solveig said after a moment, and when Osmund had left her she went to the back row of benches and sat down in the corner close to the wall of the depot. She was in no mood to explain her presence there this morning.

She had scarcely seated herself when she heard brisk steps on the walk leading from the hotel. She turned her head and saw to her dismay the last person in the world she wished to encounter at that moment. It was Morton Worthington, dressed in a well-cut light tan suit, white shirt, dark brown tie, and highly polished tan shoes, and he was whistling "Dixie" in perfect tune.

Solveig hastily turned her head away and looked at the wall of the depot. Of course he wouldn't recognize her— why should he? But there was no sense in taking any chances.

"Good morning, Miss Nordland," he said in a cheery voice. "May I introduce myself? I am Morton Worthington. My sister Patricia and I are spending the summer here —your brother may have spoken of us."

Solveig stood up and mechanically put out her hand to his extended one, but for the life of her she couldn't think of anything to say. Instead, she looked down at the none-too-attractive gingham dress she had worn that morning and blushed with embarrassment. Why hadn't she had the good sense and taste to have done better?

Morton Worthington did not seem to notice her lack of response. "Your brother said you were expecting guests on this train. We have some friends coming in from St. Louis, and I came to see if they might be arriving early."

Still Solveig stood dumb. In the distance she thought she heard the first sound of the approaching train. Then there was a cloud of black smoke as the engine came round the bend, and the people who had been gathering on the platform moved toward the tracks.

Solveig followed them. After all, one did not greet an expected guest, welcome or unwelcome, from the rear benches. The train pulled in with a roar and the bell clanged sonorously, so at least she could not be expected to make conversation with Morton Worthington.

The breathing of the engine grew lighter; the wheels under the four coaches gave a last squeak, and the train stood still. Passengers began coming out of the coaches, and Solveig held her breath. Perhaps Jordine and the children had missed the train. Such things happened, and they had to make connections from Decorah, Iowa.

The steady stream of passengers thinned to a trickle and then there were no more. "It looks as though neither of us had the good fortune of having our guests arrive," said Morton with real disappointment in his voice.

And then, out of the very front coach, came a small boy in a straw hat, his overalls faded from much scrubbing and his shirt sleeves a considerable space from his wrists. The girl just behind him had outgrown her pink-and-white checked dress, and it had been made wearable by inserting bands of some other material at the waist and at the bottom of the skirt. There was a wreath of brand-new, bright pink cotton roses around the crown of her rather battered brown straw hat, and she carried a small white crocheted bag trimmed with strange green and pink embroidery. It took some time before the brakeman helped the woman down on the platform, and she reminded Solveig of photographs she had seen of her mother and her friends taken years ago, with leg-of-mutton sleeves and heavy wide skirts. Solveig had never seen a dress like it in real life. Only the baby looked fairly presentable in its white calico dress with a white bib at its neck and a crocheted cap of some coarse thread. But the baby, too, had clumsy black shoes on its feet and heavy black ribbed stockings covering its spindly legs.

Solveig stood rooted to the spot. The fact that the little group looked scrupulously clean and that their clothes, even after the long trip, bore signs of careful pressing did not lessen her anguish. As they stood there, they looked around in anxious bewilderment.

At that moment Osmund's sharp voice came up from behind. "What's the matter with you, Solveig? Can't you see Jordine and the kids standing there on the platform?"

Could she explain to Morton that this was an old nurse who had cared for her and Osmund when they were young? But no. The thought of the smartly dressed nurses who accompanied families from the South made her reluctant to admit that Jordine had served the family even in this capacity.

"Our company did arrive," Solveig said hurriedly, and without further explanation she left him and walked swiftly down the platform.

Osmund was already holding the baby, and Jordine threw her arms around Solveig and kissed her.

"How wonderful of you both to come and meet us," she exclaimed, her voice breaking with emotion. "You are exactly like your parents. I have always said that there is no family in America as fine as the Nordlands."

"Here, Solveig," said Osmund, "you take the baby. That bag you have seems pretty heavy, Jordine. Do you have any other luggage?"

"We borrowed that from a neighbor, so we could have all our things together. And we managed very well." Jordine still retained much of the Norwegian language she had brought along with her across the Atlantic, but there was a generous enough sprinkling of English words to make herself understood.

Osmund, carrying the heavy bag, led the way to the boat. Jordine, holding a child by each hand, came next, and Solveig, carrying the baby, brought up the rear. She turned back once and caught a glimpse of Morton Worthington walking toward the hotel.

Jordine kept up a steady conversation on their way down to the lake shore. "Milda and Ragnar didn't sleep a wink all night, and the baby was restless too. I guess all of us were too excited to sleep. And by now they have already seen enough to last them all winter. They are so full of wonderful things they'll never stop talking."

Neither Ragnar nor Milda had ever been in a boat before, and all the way across the lake they sat in awed silence. The baby, in Solveig's arms, slept the entire way.

Mrs. Nordland had a hot meal ready to serve her guests as soon as they arrived, and the twins were thrilled at the arrival of two playmates. Milda and Ragnar were older than they were, but the twins could take the lead in all the games because they were on familiar ground. They had a teeter-totter which their father had set up for them on his last trip out, and there were running games on the lawn.

Astrid came racing in. "Can we take off our shoes and

stockings and go wading down by the lake shore?" she asked breathlessly.

Mrs. Nordland came out of the kitchen. "You may run barefoot up here if you wish. But no one goes down to the lake until it is time to go bathing."

"I think they should wait until tomorrow to get into the lake," Jordine said. "They have already had more than enough excitement for one day."

The children's disappointment at this news was softened a little by Sven's offering to let them watch him freeze ice cream. The children had never heard of ice cream before, and Sven let them help him pack in the ice and salt and, when it was finished, let them spoon off some of the ice cream from the dasher. It was absolutely unbelievable to Solveig that they could derive such tremendous pleasure from anything so simple.

After the evening meal Jordine and all three children showed the effects of lack of sleep. "Why don't you take them upstairs now?" asked Mrs. Nordland. "Your beds are all ready for you."

But at this Jordine showed her first resistance to anything that had been suggested. "We will sleep down here on the porch," she said with finality, "in those nice mattresses you stuffed with fresh, clean straw. We'll make up our beds at night and carry our bedding upstairs in the morning."

No amount of persuasion could make Jordine change her mind, and as Solveig went up to her own bed she had to admit that Jordine and the children were the most considerate and appreciative guests they had ever had at the lake.

If Solveig thought that Milda and Ragnar were happy

the first day, she was amazed at the ecstasy of their first swim in the lake. The twins let them borrow their water wings, and Mrs. Nordland outfitted them all with discarded clothes that they could use in the water.

Osmund and Solveig, in spite of themselves, had to admit that they had never had more fun in the water before, and they started to teach not only the children but Jordine herself how to swim. All went well until they were dressing afterward and then Jordine suddenly put her hand to her head. "My switch! Where is my switch?"

Solveig looked at her inquiringly. Then she realized that the large bun of hair that Jordine wore on top of her head was gone.

"I must have lost it in the lake," Jordine said, with complete despair in her voice. "And I'll never be able to afford another."

Solveig and Osmund got into their wet bathing suits and went back into the water. Osmund had brought two rakes from the tool shed, but all their efforts only netted them large chunks of weed.

When the swimmers were up at the house again, eating milk and cookies, Mrs. Nordland said suddenly, "Jordine, I have in mind a perfectly beautiful new hair style which I know will be most becoming to you."

Jordine looked dubious. But Mrs. Nordland curled the thin gray locks around Jordine's face with the curling iron and tucked the ends on the top of her head. It showed the natural shape of her head, and when Jordine looked at her reflection in the mirror, both front and back, she was much pleased.

"But who is going to curl it when I get back on the farm?" she asked, anxiety again in her voice.

"Tonight I am going to show you how to put the front

locks of your hair up in rags, which you can take out in the morning. It won't be difficult, and the curl will last several days. You have such pretty hair."

It was true that the new way of dressing Jordine's hair was most becoming to her, and it was amazing, Solveig thought, how much it improved her appearance.

Jordine had a supply of fairy stories that seemed inexhaustible. She would gather the twins and Milda and Ragnar about her, with little Helga in the high chair and her own baby, Mons, in her lap, and she would spin them one yarn after another. The older ones sat wide-eyed, and the two babies, soothed by the rise and fall of Jordine's voice, also seemed happy. Solveig came out on the porch when Jordine was concluding one of her tales and heard her say, "And do you know, the troll pulled a sliver from the side of the church and started down the mountainside, and immediately behind him slipped the church, with all the parishioners in their pews and the minister in his pulpit. Not even a drop of water was spilled out of the baptismal font as the church descended into the valley."

When the weather was especially pleasant, Jordine liked to spread a blanket on the soft green grass close to the shed. Sven had built a house for Arnulf's pigeons on top of his shed, where the pets had set up housekeeping. For hours Jordine and the children sat and watched the pigeons, and it got so that as soon as the blanket was spread out they would flock down to her.

On Sunday, when Solveig and her mother were preparing the evening meal in the kitchen, Solveig said suddenly, "Mamma, did you notice how Milda watched Astrid all day while she wore her pink dress? I wish we could give Milda one. Jordine keeps the children scrupulously clean, but—well, Mamma, she doesn't know much about style."

Mrs. Nordland smiled. "I had the same thought in mind. There is some pink French gingham that I had thought of making up into a dress for Astrid, but there is some other material I could use later on for her."

"I wish," said Solveig, "she could have a pair of patent-leather slippers with straps like Astrid's, too, and some white cotton stockings."

"It would mean interrupting their stay out here to go to the store," Mrs. Nordland said, "and they will be leaving for Decorah soon."

"Why couldn't you let her go barefoot tomorrow? Then I could secretly take her shoes to Mound and match the size there. They carry slippers in Pearson's store. I've seen them."

"Well," said Mrs. Nordland, "we haven't had the mail from the station since the day Jordine arrived."

"Good. Tomorrow morning I'll take the ten-o'clock train that comes from Minneapolis and goes on from Spring Park to Mound. And I'll come back on the one-thirty that goes on to Minneapolis."

When Osmund learned that Solveig was rowing across the lake he insisted on going too.

"Morton invited me to go bowling with him any time I was over there," he said, "and I can wait over between trains and do that."

Osmund was always lucky. Without planning or effort he fell into the most fortunate situations. Solveig wished she were the one, instead of Osmund, who was going to spend three hours with Morton Worthington.

But once she reached Pearson's department store in Mound she became so absorbed in her shopping that she forgot everything else. Her first purchase, of course, was to be the black patent-leather slippers. The lady clerk showed her several pairs, but either they were not the correct size or not the style Solveig wanted.

"We got some new stock in yesterday," the clerk said finally. "I'll go and see whether any of the shoe boxes have been unpacked."

She came back carrying a high tier of shoe boxes, and she and Solveig went through them together until they had narrowed the choice down to two possible pairs. One had two straps and the other four, and after much consideration Solveig settled on the four straps. They would be more suitable out in the country, and they were really prettier too.

When it came to the white cotton stockings, Solveig bought two pairs. This was to allow Milda a change. She had finished this purchase and was walking past the ribbon counter when she saw some wide pink taffeta ribbon. It was exactly the shade of the dress her mother was making for Milda. If her mother cut Milda's hair just as she did Astrid's, a bow of this ribbon would look beautiful on it.

But she had already spent more than her mother had figured on. The slippers were more expensive, and so were the extra pair of stockings. She still had some change left from what her mother had given her, but that didn't mean she could spend all of it. Well, she had brought along some of her own money. The hair ribbon could be a present from her.

But wasn't there something else she was supposed to get? Solveig tried to think. The large clock on the wall told her she would have to be leaving for the station.

She stood still at the door. It would be terrible to go home without completing her errands.

Then it came to her—a pair of overalls for Ragnar. She hurried over to the boys' and men's furnishings, and since she knew the size the transaction was made in a hurry. At the station her train was just ready to leave, and Solveig sank into her seat, breathless but triumphant.

The next day when Milda was dressed in her new clothes she bore only a slight resemblance to the awkward, pale child that Solveig had seen step off the train. The patent-leather slippers and white stockings fit her perfectly, and the wide taffeta bow in her short hair exactly matched the pink dress over the lovely white petticoat that Mrs. Nordland had also sewed for her.

"Your papa isn't going to recognize his little girl when he meets us at the depot," Jordine said.

Although the change in Ragnar was not nearly as great, he looked much improved with a close haircut and the new overalls. Even the baby, in one of Helga's plainer but very good dresses and white stockings and shoes she had outgrown, seemed different and sweeter.

Clothes certainly make a difference, Solveig thought. It was hard to believe that she could ever have been ashamed of poor, sweet Jordine and those really lovable children. She didn't like to think what Morton Worthington must have thought of her, but she wished he could have been at the station today to get a better impression both of her and of the kind of guests the family entertained.

CHAPTER SIX

SOLVEIG sat back in the comfortable chair and rocked
luxuriously. It seemed too good to be true. Here she was,
sitting like a lady of leisure on the Swensons' porch,
dressed in one of her best summer dresses and with
absolutely nothing to do but to enjoy herself.

Serene Swenson's invitation to spend the weekend
with her could not have arrived at a more opportune
time. Solveig and her mother were catching their breath
after Jordine's departure, and they had decided to postpone getting the household back to normal for a few
days. Serene's parents were visiting relatives in Duluth,
and since Solveig had been working so hard, Mrs. Nordland said that the change would do her good. Serene
was almost the same age as Solveig, and her two brothers
were not much younger.

The Swensons kept a maid winter and summer, and

so Serene always looked as though she were dressed for an important engagement. Today she had on a navy blue silk, and with her dark hair and brown eyes she might have posed for the cover of a magazine. Her figure, too, was perfect—tall and slim, with shapely legs and ankles. Solveig was never so aware of the shortcomings of her own appearance as when she was with Serene.

Now, as Solveig sat rocking and Serene was manicuring her fingernails, the maid came in carrying a tray.

"Set it down on the marble-top table, Katna," said Serene, "and we'll help ourselves."

After she was gone Serene said, "I wish Katna would bake the kind of rusks your mother makes instead of feeding us those she orders by the barrel." But Solveig noticed, nevertheless, that Serene helped herself to four of the out-of-the-barrel rusks.

When they were finished, Serene brought out a comb and brush and mirror and proceeded to fuss with her hair.

"I'm trying to decide on a new hairdo," she told Solveig. "I've noticed several that the ladies at the hotel are wearing, and they look stunning."

She braided and unbraided her hair. She rolled it on her fingers and pinned tiny rolls here and there. She piled all the hair in a great mound on top of her head, and with each operation she viewed her reflection in the hand mirror. At first Solveig was interested, but after a while she became bored.

"I think I'd like to read something," she told Serene. "What have you got to read that's good?"

Serene yawned. "The boys have some sort of detective stories around here," she said, "but they keep them hidden. The family doesn't like them to read such stuff."

Solveig got up and went inside. There must be books

or magazines somewhere around. But all she found was a Bible and a hymnbook, both of them in Norwegian. She opened the Bible but found the Norwegian such slow going that she laid it down again. When she returned to the porch, Serene was combing her hair back into the fashion she usually wore.

"When we move back to Minneapolis this fall, I'm going to ask Mamma if I can't go to a professional hairdresser and have her teach me a good style," Serene said.

"I'd feel foolish going to one," Solveig admitted. "The only person I ever heard of who went to a hairdresser was Carrie Aamoth's aunt, and that was after she married that rich man from New York."

"I'll catch a rich man," said Serene. "At least I expect to after I've seen one."

Solveig again sat watching Serene work with her nails. Finally, after consulting her mirror, Serene said, "Let's go for a boat ride." Solveig had already had one boat ride that day, coming over to the Swensons', but she welcomed any activity that would relieve her of watching Serene fuss with herself.

Down by the shore Serene asked, "Don't you want to do the rowing? I feel sort of tired today."

Solveig wondered what could have tired Serene, but she didn't mind rowing. After all, she was embarking on a carefree boat ride before noon, something she had always envied others doing. At about this time at home she would probably be washing floors.

Serene stretched out luxuriously in the back seat. "Do you know," she said, "next year I'm going to have a real bathing suit made by our dressmaker, and I've planned exactly how it's going to look. I'll coax Mother to buy bright red broadcloth, and, believe me, it will take a lot of coaxing to get a really bright red. It will have a deep neck and no sleeves at all, and that will take some maneuvering too. I'd like panties of the same material, and the skirt will only be just below the knees. I'm going to have to start working on the project right after Christmas to get Mother convinced and the suit finished by the time we move to the lake in the spring."

Serene continued to chatter on. It seemed that her mind was full of clothes that she would wear in and out of the water. The wind had gone down and the lake was as unruffled as a looking glass. And the sun was sending down more and more heat.

"I think I'd like to return to shore," Solveig heard herself say. How could she really be the person to make such a suggestion, now that she was enjoying one of her most cherished dreams?

Serene yawned. "All right. Katna should have dinner ready by now. I hope she's made something good."

When they came into the house, Katna greeted them: "The least you children could do would be to be on hand for meals."

"Didn't the boys come back?" Serene asked.

"I haven't seen them." But in spite of her short manner she gave them sausages and pancakes and cleared the table after they had finished.

After Solveig and Serene were back on the porch, Serene explained that her brothers would be bringing back a friend with them when they came from the station. His name was Donald Brown, and her brother, Ludvig, had reported that he was a perfect scream. He knew no end of card tricks and other kinds of fun, and Serene had been dying to meet him.

Solveig, too, welcomed the prospect of the arrival of

the boys. So far her visit had been anything but exciting, but with the arrival of Donald Brown things were bound to improve.

At three o'clock there was no sign of the boys, and Serene suggested a game of croquet. Solveig was very much impressed to discover that the Swensons had a real croquet ground made of smooth, hard earth pounded down, with a ridge around it to keep the balls from rolling away. But in a little while she realized that she was at a distinct disadvantage. At home she had to give the ball a harder push on the grass to make it travel. Here she invariably shot past her mark, and she lost game after game. When Serene said she was tired of playing, Solveig made no objection.

"I guess Donald Brown has too many important friends to be bothered to come over here," Serene said sadly, and just then the younger of the Swenson boys, Bjorn, came running up the path from the lake shore.

"How did you get here?" Serene demanded. "We've been watching for the boat for hours."

"Donald wanted us to row close to shore. We landed a lot of times, and you should see all the great things he can do. He can climb and jump up in trees just like a monkey."

"Where are the boys now?"

"Down by the landing. They want you girls to come down to the lake."

Serene gave her hair a few extra pats, and they all started down the path to the lake shore.

"He says he's going to show you some real sport on the lake," Bjorn said.

Solveig felt a slight misgiving at this news. From earliest childhood she and all the other children of her family had been warned against cutting any capers while they were out on the lake. But, after all, she had been envying the neighbors for the fun they were having, and now that she was getting the same chance herself she certainly was not going to spoil it by being a wet blanket.

Donald Brown was an overgrown boy in his middle teens with a crop of unruly brown hair only a little darker than the skin of his round face. He greeted the girls effusively. "So pleased to have the pleasure of your company," he said. "It is a pleasure to be entertaining you for a little while."

He was especially attentive to Serene and insisted that she sit beside him on the front rower's seat of the boat. Solveig he placed in the back seat and the younger Swenson boy, Bjorn, in the extreme front.

"To begin with," he told the older Swenson boy, Ludvig, "you will do the rowing.

"Row straight out toward the middle of the lake," Donald Brown commanded after the boat was well away from shore.

Ludvig did as he was told.

"My brothers say you can do all sorts of tricks," Serene said, blushing. "They think you're wonderful."

"They haven't seen anything yet," said Donald Brown, with no trace of modesty in his voice.

After Ludvig had rowed about one third the distance across the lake, Donald Brown gave the command for him to stop.

"Move over so you sit just behind Serene," he told Ludvig.

Then, to Solveig's dismay, Donald Brown stood straight up in the boat. He waved his hands, raised one foot, stepped over his side of the boat, and plunged down beside Ludvig. As he did so the boat veered, letting in a plop of water. Solveig gasped but managed to suppress the exclamation that almost escaped her lips. In all her life she had never seen anyone stand up in a boat, much less hop around as Donald Brown had just done.

"Now listen to me," Donald Brown told Ludvig. "You are about to participate in the aquatic act called Wiggle the Worm."

Serene giggled.

"I'll take two strokes with my oar, and the minute I've done this, you follow with two strokes from yours. But you have to do it quick as lightning and pull with all your might, or the worm won't wiggle."

Solveig knew enough about rowing to realize what the effect of this procedure would be, and her surmises were only too correct. Scarcely had Donald given his two strokes than the boat lurched violently to one side. And with Ludvig following suit, the boat turned just as crazily to the other. Spray began to descend on everyone, and Solveig held her breath. With every new turn she was sure the boat would tip. Serene giggled hysterically.

"Don't do that any more," the younger Swenson boy cried out. "I almost fell out of the boat."

"Had enough, Serene?" Donald Brown asked.

"Yes," she managed to say. Then she added hastily, "It's wonderful."

Solveig felt ashamed that she was too cowardly to let Donald Brown know how disgusted she felt with him. Suppose the little fellow up front had been dumped into the lake, what then? On the other hand, she was out for fun now for once in her life, and she hated to have the boys think she was a softy.

"We might as well try Whirling the Wheel," Donald

Brown said. Again he stood up in the boat, stepped over the back rower's seat, and sat down. "Hand me an oar," he told Ludvig.

The older brother obeyed. Donald Brown fastened it down on his side of the boat.

"Now," he told Ludvig, "just keep rowing. And put some real spark into your oar. With only one to manage, you should be able to do a good job of it."

Solveig was terrified. For, as Donald Brown gave this command, he had Ludvig move to the same side of the boat he was sitting on. The terrific rowing would spin the boat around like a top. And, with the rather strong wind that had suddenly blown up out in the middle of the lake, the chance of the boat staying right side up was practically nil.

"You can't do that," she finally found the voice to say.

But Donald Brown laughed at her and gave his oar a hard pull.

Solveig could only close her eyes and hang on with both hands. She could hear water pouring into the boat, and she was not sure half the time if the boat was right side up or overturned.

A whimper from Bjorn pulled Solveig out of her lethargy. Leaning forward, she seized Donald Brown's arm. "Don't you dare take another stroke," she yelled, and at that moment the older Swenson boy stopped rowing too.

"Fraidy cat," Donald Brown sneered.

"Serene," Solveig said, "make him take us back to shore. And tell your brothers you've had enough of Donald Brown's tricks."

There was an expression of unmistakable relief on Serene's face, and Bjorn stopped his whimpering. But

Solveig knew that she alone would be considered the wet blanket of the party. And, as a matter of fact, she didn't much care. Donald Brown wasn't worth worrying about, and the rest were lucky to have escaped with their lives.

Donald Brown sat in sullen silence all the way back to the shore. When they reached the house the maid announced supper, but he refused to stay. He'd take the road around the lake home, he said. He had a date for the evening. And no one pressed him to change his mind.

After supper the maid went upstairs to her room as soon as she had washed the dishes.

"Well, I suppose we might as well turn in too," said Serene.

Solveig felt really disappointed. At home, the evenings after the younger children had been tucked into bed were the coziest time of the day. Often her mother made a cool drink or served cookies or fruit, and the family read or visited. But she had nothing to suggest, and so she followed Serene upstairs and went into the room that was to be hers overnight.

Solveig did not start to bed immediately after she had closed her door, for she felt both lonely and a little nervous in the large, dark, quiet house. Finally she started to undress, taking off one garment after the other with long pauses in between, made her way over to the bed, and blew out the light.

With the darkness all around her the house seemed lonelier and emptier than ever. It was so close to the water that Solveig could hear the lapping of the waves and the grinding sound of the boat as it rubbed against the dock. And there were strange sounds in the woods too. Insects kept up a constant chorus; frogs croaked; there was a loud hooting of an owl, and overhead on the roof it sounded as though a race of some kind was taking place.

Suddenly Solveig stiffened in fright. There was a rustling just outside her door and then a creaking on the steps leading down to the dining room. This was no figment of her imagination. There was someone roaming about in the house. Had Donald Brown, angry at the way he had been treated, returned for revenge? Had someone heard that Mr. and Mrs. Swenson were away and come to rob the place? Or was it haunted?

Frightened as she was, Solveig decided that this last idea was ridiculous. And if intruders were about, it was up to her to discover them.

Her heart was beating wildly as she got out of bed. Without waiting to dress or even to put on her shoes she walked across the bedroom floor and softly opened the door leading into the hall. Then she stopped to listen. All was quiet now. She tiptoed out into the hall and again stood still. Again all was quiet.

The first thing to do was to make sure that the Swenson children were safe. Slowly she made her way to the door of Serene's room, next to hers. The door was open. Solveig walked in and over to the bed, and to her horror she found it empty. She looked under the bed. No one was there.

Now thoroughly alarmed, Solveig went to the bedroom she knew the boys occupied. That door, too, was open, and the bed was empty.

For a moment Solveig stood rooted to the spot, overcome by panic. Then she began to try to use reason. No single person could have made off with all three children by force without arousing the household, and if there were several intruders they, too, would have caused considerable commotion. The most likely conclusion was that all three of the Swensons had left under their own power, and if so they must still be close by. Solveig wished now that she had gotten up at once instead of giving way to her fears and hesitating so long. Well, she would hesitate no longer, scared as she still was.

The stairs creaked as she went down, but the maid was evidently a sound sleeper and there was no movement in her room. Groping her way through the dark, Solveig reached the porch and found that the screen door was unhooked. She opened it and went down the steps and touched the cool, damp ground with her bare feet.

Then, out in the darkness, she saw a single light. It was in the direction of the Swensons' boathouse and moved about as though someone was swinging it. The last thing Solveig wanted to do at that moment was to walk down to the lake shore. If she stopped to look or listen, there were enough objects and sounds to frighten her out of her wits. Well, she had better not look or listen. Standing still and counting to three, she mustered all the courage she had. Then she started out, almost at a run, for the spot from which the light had come.

As she drew near the boathouse she slowed down, and she had almost reached the lake when she heard voices, subdued yet unmistakable.

"Are you sure it isn't dangerous, with all that fizz in it?" It was Serene who was asking the question.

"Sure," Ludvig said. "We each of us had a bottle of it over at the station. We didn't get sick. And it tasted grand. It's called pop."

"Did Donald Brown buy it for you?" Serene asked.

"No. He used our money."

Solveig could see them now. They were all three crouched down by the shore end of their short dock, and Ludvig was holding the bottles.

"He used all our money," Bjorn said. "Now I haven't enough for church tomorrow."

"Never mind about church," said Serene. "I'll give you some of mine. Hurry up and open the bottles so I can taste it."

"Donald Brown gave us a thing to open them with. Gee, I'll bet he'll be mad when he remembers he left it. We were going to have a midnight party tonight."

Solveig had heard enough. Turning around, before she was discovered, she made for the house as fast as she could. Her feet were cold and wet when she got into bed, and she could only think with pity about the Swenson children.

Their parents held them down so strictly that not even Serene had heard of a common drink like pop. At home, while her father and mother held the children accountable for what they did, they never had to resort to secrecy when they had a new experience. To be sure, Osmund was a little older than the Swenson boys, but even so she couldn't imagine his having to resort to midnight trips down to the lake. He would most likely have brought some of the pop home, or anything else that was new, and treated the household openly and generously with it.

Solveig woke up late on Sunday morning and was barely in time for breakfast. The boys were dressed in their best and sat with scrubbed faces and wet hair pasted to their heads. Serene's dress was of silk.

There was almost no conversation at the table. And when the meal was over the maid said, "Be sure to come straight back from church. I want to get the dishes done after dinner in time for a good long nap in the afternoon."

Before leaving for church Serene did not bother to fuss with her hair or to perfect the manicure of her fingernails. Evidently much of the preening yesterday was in anticipation of the exciting youth her brothers had promised to bring home with them.

At the church service the three Swenson children sat side by side, the picture of Sabbath decorum. Solveig heard whispered remarks about how well they had been brought up. Even in the absence of their parents they behaved perfectly all the time and were an example for other young people to follow.

It was late in the afternoon when Solveig returned to her own home, and Pan was the first one to greet her. He ran out on the dock, jumped up on her, almost pushing her into the lake, and licked her face. The twins came running down the hill, and each one took one of Solveig's hands and held it tight. So much of importance had happened to them both since she left, and they interrupted each other so often, that she was not able to understand either of them. Up on the porch, little Helga stretched out her arms to Solveig and her mother kissed her.

Osmund waited until the excitement was over and then he drawled, "Welcome home, Miss Dishwasher. The knives and forks and plates and cups and saucers have missed you."

"I'm pleased to know that you're the spokesman for the dishes," Solveig retorted. "And since you seem to be on such intimate terms with them, I won't deprive you of the honor and pleasure of your new role."

"I hate to disappoint you," said Osmund, "but I resigned from the duty just before you arrived. I wouldn't for the world separate my sweet sister from anything for which she is so admirably fitted."

Solveig picked up the dipper to sprinkle him with water, and Osmund fled from the kitchen.

CHAPTER SEVEN

Solveig woke up the next morning with a feeling of something hanging over her. Then she remembered that this was the day her mother had set aside for doing the tremendous wash that had accumulated during the visit of Jordine and the children.

On her way home yesterday Solveig had had visions of spending the whole day reading. She would supply herself with ears of corn, if any were left over after their meal, with a salt shaker; or stalks of rhubarb with sugar; or whatever other snack was at hand to chew while devouring the books and magazines that had accumulated.

Instead her mother had asked her to help collect the soiled clothes—and there were piles and piles of them. They had carried them out to the west side of the house, sorted them, soaked the white clothes in soapsuds, and gotten out the washing paraphernalia. And now, at dawn, this terrible wash was waiting for her and her mother.

Reluctantly Solveig got out of bed and dressed. She couldn't let her mother get breakfast and also start the wash. If she did, things would drag on and on.

Outside, on the west side of the house, Solveig took deep breaths of the fresh morning air. If this gigantic wash hadn't been staring her in the face, she would actually have enjoyed being out here. She couldn't help but be aware how fresh it was this morning, perfect weather for a washday. And she couldn't help but be glad that it could be done outdoors instead of in the hot kitchen.

Sven had already kindled a brisk fire in the rusty old stove, which had served its purpose faithfully as far back as Solveig could remember. A thin line of smoke rose out of its pipe, which was open at the top. And when Solveig lifted the lid of the boiler she found that the soapy water which she and her mother had put in the night before was already hot and ready to be poured into the washing machine.

But Solveig did not do this immediately. Instead she put the lid back on the boiler and stood still.

It was so lovely. Only a slight breeze from the south brushed against her cheek. It smelled of fresh water, and she took deep breaths. On the other side of the road Lily greeted her with a long moo, and Solveig heard her cowbell ringing with every movement she made. In the city Lily's bell would have disturbed the neighbors. But as soon as she arrived in her pasture at the lake, she was belled and actually seemed to enjoy it.

Overhead a crow flew by, cawing for all it was worth, as if to announce that she was not the only one who rose at the brink of dawn. Something she and Osmund called a scissors bug sent out sharp sounds from a nearby tree, and there was a chorus of birds from almost everywhere on the place.

The west wall of the woodshed was a mass of pink hollyhocks, and the wooden cover of the cesspool was purple with morning glories. Toward the front of this part of the yard a bed of orange-red tiger lilies stood in bloom, from early spring until the family moved to the city. No one ever picked a tiger-lily blossom, or for that matter seemed to pay any attention to them, but they were always there. So was a bed of smelling grass which Mrs. Nordland called by the Norwegian name *renfang*. The leaves resembled forest ferns in shape, but they were heavier and a darker green and they had a most pungent odor. This year the west side of the house was made even more attractive by the addition of a patch of glorious nasturtiums. Early in the spring Mr. Nordland had thrown a package of seeds on last year's ash pile, and the results had been astounding.

Solveig was brought back from her daydreaming by a rapping on the kitchen window.

"Hadn't you better get started, dear?" her mother called out to her.

Of course. No one did a big washing by staring at the landscape. But it was a pity to leave off enjoying so much beauty and turn instead to a mess of soiled clothing.

The tall washing machine was new that year and really quite imposing. A fairly large cube-like metal case was held in place by four sturdy wooden legs. Inside there was a cylinder-like container in which the clothes were actually washed, and this was achieved by turning a crank that was fastened outside. Solveig had to admit that it was going to be quite a relief not to rub clothes on the washboard any more.

Soon the steaming suds had been transferred into the washing machine, the boiler filled by turning on the faucet and holding the hose down inside it. Then Solveig started to turn the crank of the washing machine, and by the time tantalizing odors of freshly boiled coffee and frying fish wafted out through the kitchen window she had the first lot of clothes washed and boiling in the boiler, the second lot ready to go into the machine, and all three tubs of rinsing water filled from the water hose.

"Breakfast is ready," her mother called out to her. The invitation was a most welcome one, for Solveig had worked up a tremendous appetite.

There was fresh fried fish with cream poured over it and pocketbook rolls and fresh butter and strawberry jam and fragrant, steaming coffee with more cream. How did her mother manage? Solveig wondered. Little Helga was sitting in her high chair, all bathed and dressed and looking as fresh as a daisy, and her mother still had time to stop and fix the arm of Astrid's doll, where the sawdust was leaking.

"The Sathers are washing today too," Mrs. Nordland said. "Edith was up just now and wondered if we couldn't have a wash party together."

Solveig was pleased. Usually there was a wash party every week, but there had been no regular washday during Jordine's visit, and so it hadn't been convenient.

Solveig insisted that her mother remain indoors until it was time to starch and hang up the clothes. And after this was finished she and Osmund washed all the laundry paraphernalia with great care and set it out in the sun to dry. When they were through it was past noon, and Solveig was wonderfully hungry again in spite of the big breakfast she had eaten.

Astrid came running at breakneck speed around the side of the house. "The wash party is all ready, and you're both supposed to come right away," she yelled.

It was a welcome sight that greeted Solveig and Osmund when they reached the east lawn. Under the huge oak that stood a little distance from the house a white tablecloth had been spread out on the ground. Around it were gathered the women and children of the Nordland and Sather families. Even little Helga was perched on a pillow beside the tablecloth and propped up with several more. Mrs. Nordland was dishing up cold chicken and potato salad. and Edith Sather was passing the full plates around.

"Whew!" Osmund exclaimed. "This is a real shindig."

The two Sather boys came through the gate and sat down beside the two Nordland boys.

"Who made all the food?" Solveig wanted to know.

"Mamma made the potato salad yesterday when you were gone, and I helped her with it," Astrid volunteered.

"And Sven and I froze the ice cream this morning," Arnulf put in.

"Tattletale," Astrid said. "That was supposed to be a surprise."

"But it's time for the surprise right now," her mother reminded her. Then she added, "But the Sathers have contributed as much and more than we have. Mrs. Sather fried the chicken, and Edith baked the popovers."

"And she's baked thousands of them so we can have all we want," said Arnulf, pushing a mountainous one into his mouth.

"And the Sathers are furnishing the coffee," Mrs. Nordland said.

"But don't think we don't appreciate the milk and cream from the Nordland dairy," Mrs. Sather added.

Just then Sven came walking up the road.

"Here comes the ice-cream man," the youngest Sather boy called out.

"I was wondering if it's time to take the root beer down to the icehouse," said Sven.

"We haven't mixed and bottled it yet," said Solveig. "And, anyway, it's time for you to eat now."

After the ice cream had been eaten and the party was over, Sven, Osmund, and Solveig went back to the west side of the house. Solveig measured the root-beer mixture carefully and stirred both vats until she was sure everything had been properly mixed and dissolved. Then Osmund filled each bottle, and Solveig clamped its patent top securely and handed it to Sven. Sven laid each one in the wheelbarrow in such a way that there would be no danger of any of them rolling off when he wheeled them down the hill to the icehouse.

"It comes out just right every week," Solveig said finally. "Two dozen quart bottles as usual."

"There are still a few left from last week," said Sven. "I noticed when I filled the icebox this morning."

"That's good. It's better when it's had a chance to age a little."

"It won't get a chance to age long, I guess," said Sven. "I heard Arnulf teasing his mother to let him and the Sather kids fill their glasses with it after she had put a spoonful of ice cream in each. What kids here in America don't think of!"

When the bottles were all put away in the cool, damp sawdust of the icehouse, Osmund said that he and the Sather boys were going to row over to the hotel for the mail. Solveig would have liked to go along. It would have been good, after her strenuous morning, just to sit back in the boat. And it might even have been possible to see the Worthingtons, who might very well happen to be in the lobby of the hotel or out on the grounds.

Instead Solveig helped her mother take the clothes down from the lines—they had strung the whole yard west of the house with extra ones. She helped to fold and press and put away the flat pieces and sprinkle the others that needed real ironing.

Finally her mother said, "Why don't you go out on the front porch and read the last issue of the *Ladies' Home Journal?* We're going to have waffles for supper, and only one of us will have to watch the waffle iron. Astrid can set the table. It is time she learns to do her part instead of playing all the time."

"But aren't you tired?" Solveig asked.

"You did most of the heavy work today," Mrs. Nordland said, smiling.

The appetizing fragrance of the waffles came out to Solveig, as she lay curled up in the hammock, reading, and she thought what a really good day it had been. She was still in this mellow mood when Osmund and the two Sather nephews came up on the porch. The Sathers proudly displayed two large pickerel strung on a willow branch which they held between them.

"Osmund let me help him pull in this one," the younger of the two said. "And he's letting me take it down to Aunt Edith to cook."

"I did almost all the rowing," the older one said.

"I couldn't have gotten along without either of you," Osmund said. Then he turned to Solveig. "We met Morton and Patricia up at the hotel. They want us to fix a date when we can spend the entire day with them. Morton says that before we know it the summer will be over and they'll be going back to St. Louis."

"You're fooling!" said Solveig.

"What do you mean, fooling?"

"The Worthingtons have such elegant friends at the hotel. They wouldn't want to spend a whole day with us."

"Don't be silly. They're nice young kids. Besides, we're as good as they are."

"You're always so sure of yourself, Osmund."

"There's no reason why I shouldn't be. Now, do you want to accept their invitation or don't you?"

"Of course, I'd love to go."

"Well, then, when? They wanted to know."

"We'll have to do some planning first," said Solveig wildly. "What on earth would you wear?"

"My Sunday suit," said Osmund promptly.

"It's too tight," said Solveig. She went out on the back porch where her mother was shelling peas, and Osmund followed her. Mrs. Nordland listened carefully while the whole matter was explained to her.

"I see no reason why Osmund shouldn't get a new suit. I've been thinking so for some time. He will be needing it when school opens."

"Can he go to town tomorrow and buy it?" Solveig asked eagerly. "The Worthingtons want to know when we can come."

Mrs. Nordland shook her head. "Your father is in Chicago this week and won't be back until Saturday. And then he wants to spend the following Monday out here supervising some transplanting that Sven is going to do. So I'm afraid Osmund will have to wait until a week from Tuesday to buy his suit."

Solveig looked anxiously toward Osmund. "Do you think that will be too late? Wednesday, I mean? The day after you have bought your suit?"

Osmund smiled. "I think it will be all right. The Worthingtons only want to be sure we set a day aside before they leave for Missouri."

"I think it will be very nice for you both to have a visit with them," Mrs. Nordland said. "From what I have heard about them, they seem to be fine young people."

All evening Solveig could think of nothing else. It seemed too good to be true. She had always felt the elegant guests at the luxurious hotel lived in a world which she could never enter, and now, out of a clear sky, she was invited to become a part of it. It was really fortunate that she and Osmund had a week to get used to the idea and to do all the planning and preparing that would be necessary before the important day arrived.

CHAPTER EIGHT

It seemed to Solveig that she had never been so hot in her life. She stopped ironing Osmund's best white shirt to mop her face and neck and to try and decide which was hotter—the kitchen where the wood stove was going full blast to heat the heavy irons and to bake the bread her mother was making, or the back porch where the afternoon sun had forced its scorching rays through the west end.

A lucky dog, Osmund, Solveig thought, as she bent over the ironing board again. Here he was spending the day in town with Papa, getting outfitted with a new suit of clothes, and very likely being taken to a fine, cool restaurant and getting treated to a tempting lunch. Boys in a family had the edge on girls every time.

Finally the bottom of what had been a heaping clothesbasket was in sight. Only the neckbands and cuffs of her father's and brother's shirts needed cold-starching, and that at least was a cooler operation. Solveig mixed the starch in a bowl, dipped the neckbands and cuffs into it, and then wrapped them all in a large bath towel. They would come out better in the ironing if they were allowed to lie awhile, and in the meantime she could take a breathing spell on the front porch.

"Do you think you could keep the twins out there with you for a while?" called her mother. "I don't like them running outdoors in such a hot sun, and they are cross already."

Solveig heaved a sigh of disappointment. Gone was the respite of a few minutes of rest. But caring for the children and doing the baking must have been an even more trying struggle on this torrid day than her ironing had been.

Luckily Sven had brought up to the house a bushel basket full of unhusked sweet corn. Solveig took a half dozen of the shapely ones and helped Astrid dress them up in her doll clothes. She opened the husks at the top and drew out the corn silk. This she showed Astrid how to braid and tie up with bits of leftover baby ribbon that was used to thread through the beading of little Helga's dresses. It was such a novel idea that Astrid settled down happily to the hair dressing.

It took a little more imagination to find something for Arnulf to do, but some cattails solved the problem. Solveig cut them a short distance up from the stem and set them on squares of cardboard, holding them upright with a little melted candle wax.

"Now you can have the cattails for men and women and play soldier with them," she told Arnulf. "And here are some paper boxes which can be wagons or boats. The cattail people can ride in them and be passengers, or they can be policemen or trainmen or anything else you want them to be."

When the twins were playing quietly, helped by root beer and cookies, Solveig went to see if she could help to start supper. Her father and Osmund were going to be tired and hungry after their long day in the city.

"I have a lemon filling to put between the cake layers," her mother said. "We'll whip the cream for the top just before we serve it tonight. By the way, how are the beans and the ham doing in the oven?"

"I've just looked at them," said Solveig, "and they look good. I basted a little more of the brown-sugar-and-raisin mixture over the ham just now. And everything is ready for the potato salad."

"I hope your father had no trouble finding a suit for Osmund," Mrs. Nordland said. "They certainly struck a terribly hot day to spend in the city."

At that moment Pan whimpered as he stood by the door, begging to be allowed in the kitchen. Solveig let him in, and he went at once to the ironing board and crouched under it.

"What do you suppose is the matter with him?" Solveig asked. "Pan doesn't usually act like this."

She had scarcely finished speaking when there was a distant but prolonged roar of thunder.

"There must be a storm coming," Mrs. Nordland said. "Pan is dreadfully afraid of thunder and lightning. But the sky in the east is blue. The storm can't be that close."

"It's a good thing Papa and Osmund planned to take the first train," said Solveig. "Otherwise they might have been caught in it."

Again there was thunder, this time louder and clearer.

"Solveig, go out in front and see how the sky looks to the northwest," her mother said. "We always get our worst storms from that direction."

"Mamma, it's getting darker already," Solveig said as she went toward the front of the house, and then she ran back again. "Mamma, the whole sky toward the west is pitch black, and——"

There was a flash of lightning and a deafening roar of thunder.

"Quick, Solveig, get the twins inside, and I'll carry Helga's high chair into the dining room."

There was a wild scramble getting in the movable things from the porch.

"I'll go upstairs and close the windows," Mrs. Nordland said. "Solveig, you close those downstairs and the door."

Pan slunk under the dining-room table and whimpered.

It grew so dark that it was hard to see anything. Helga started to cry, and Solveig picked her up from the high chair and held her in her arms.

Mrs. Nordland came downstairs. "I'm afraid this is going to be a real storm," she said.

"Aren't we going down in the storm cellar?" Arnulf asked.

"There is no time to get there now," his mother said.

The flashes of lightning were almost continuous now and followed by roar after roar of thunder. And it sounded as though the wind was tearing the timbers of the house apart.

"I want to go and take in my pigeons," said Arnulf tearfully.

"I am sure they have all gone into their house by now," his mother told him.

"But, Mamma," Solveig said, "Papa and Osmund——"

Her voice was drowned out by a clap of thunder so terrific that the entire house shook.

"Mamma, I'm scared," Astrid said tearfully.

Lightning that resembled illuminated wire was almost constant now, and the thunder followed instantly like shots from a cannon.

"Solveig, keep Helga in your arms. And here are chairs for you, Astrid and Arnulf, near Solveig. It is best to keep away from the walls and the windows."

"But you, Mamma?" Solveig asked.

"I am going to see how the lake looks," Mrs. Nordland said.

While she was away the rain came—hard, forceful, violent rain. Solveig and the children could hear it pound on the roof upstairs and against the walls and windows on the west side where the house was unprotected by porches.

Mrs. Nordland returned, and through the flashes of lightning Solveig could see that her mother was deadly pale.

"How is it, Mamma?" Solveig asked.

"The lake was a mass of black waves when I first looked out. Now it is impossible to see any farther than the porch."

She sank into a chair beside Astrid.

"Won't Papa and Osmund ever come back any more?" Astrid asked.

"God will take care of them and bring them back safely to us," Mrs. Nordland said.

"Mamma, take Helga for a moment," Solveig said. "I want to see whether the rain is coming through the west window. All the baking is on the table close to it, and it's raining so hard it might be seeping in."

As she came into the kitchen, Solveig felt as though

she was being fenced in by fire. With one hard pull she managed to yank the table away from the window.

"Mamma," she called hoarsely, "I'm afraid the lightning is going to strike the chimney. It's terrible out here."

"Come and sit down again with us," her mother told her quietly. "God is with us even during a storm."

Her quiet manner calmed all the children. While the lightning flashed out of the inky darkness and the thunder sounded with earsplitting intensity and the wind shook the house and the rain beat down in torrents, the children sat without uttering a whimper, reassured as they were by their mother's trustful calmness.

After what seemed like hours the wire-like lightning became less frequent and the lightning flashes less glaring. There were longer intervals between each clap of thunder, and the wind lost a little of its fury. The rain slowed into a steady downpour, and it was possible to see beyond the screen of the porches.

"Solveig," Mrs. Nordland said, "I'm going to put an old raincoat over my head and go out to take a look at the weather. Stay here with the children and don't let any of them move until I come back."

"But, Mamma, is it safe?" Solveig protested.

Her mother did not answer. The slamming of the outside front door told Solveig that she had left the house.

Gradually daylight returned, so that the lightning was not as startling as it had been during the total darkness. The thunder became a rumbling roar, receding farther and farther into the distance. It continued to rain but more gently, and the wind no longer beat against the house.

"Isn't Mamma ever coming back?" Astrid asked fearfully.

"Of course," Solveig said, doing her best to imitate her mother's calm manner. She was sorely tempted to go out on the porch and see what had happened, but her mother's parting admonition stayed her.

Then the front door opened and her mother came into the house, dripping wet. Her face was pale, and for the first time it registered actual fear.

"It has been a terrible storm," was all she would say.

Then suddenly, loud and clear so that there could be no mistaking the sound of Deering's whistle came through the open door. Toot, toot, toot, it came again. This time Solveig didn't wait for her mother's permission. With one leap she was out of her chair, and without stopping to put on anything to protect her from the rain she tore out of doors. Over the wet lawns, down the hill, and out on the slippery dock she flew.

There it was, only partly visible through the still falling rain—Deering's bright red steamer. Solveig strained her eyes. At first she could not see what passengers were aboard. Then there was the flutter of a white handkerchief. It was Osmund, and close beside him was her father. Solveig couldn't see anything after that. This time it was not because of the darkness and the rain but because her eyes were filled with tears.

Somehow she and her father and Osmund got up the hill from the lake, and then the entire family was together inside the parlor. What happened after that became so firmly imprinted on Solveig's mind that she knew she would not forget it if she lived to be a hundred.

She had always known her father as rather stern and certainly reserved and dignified. But he wrapped his arms around her mother and kissed her again and again. He picked up little Helga and tossed her high in the air, and every time she came down he gave her a big hug and a prolonged kiss. After that he showered the twins with kisses, and finally he came to Solveig. With tears still on his cheeks he said brokenly, "Thank God, my wonderful daughter, that I find you all here and safe." And he held her to him for a long time.

All this while Osmund stood silent. But after little Helga came down for the last time, Osmund took her in his arms and cradled her as carefully as though she might have been a china doll he was afraid of breaking.

To Solveig's surprise, it was her mother, tender and loving as she always was, who remained outwardly calm. It was she who finally suggested to her husband that he tell how Captain Deering and all his passengers managed to survive the storm.

The air had been unusually oppressive when the train pulled into the Spring Park station, but there had been no indication of an immediate storm. Down by the lake a ridge of clouds was gathering in the west, but it was not until the steamer was halfway between the station and the point that it was evident that bad weather was on the way. Captain Deering made all possible speed, hoping to put in at Fagerness until the storm was over. But by the time the steamer reached the dock there the wind was so terrific that it dashed the steamer against it. The dock crumbled like an eggshell, but fortunately the boat was not damaged.

"I'll have to steer straight into the wind," Captain Deering said.

Solveig's father did not go into detail about the storm on the lake except to say that the waves sometimes washed so high on the deck that it seemed certain the boat would go under.

"I was very proud of our Osmund," Mr. Nordland said. "Without being foolishly optimistic about our chances, he helped to calm the women and children during the worst of the storm as though he were a veteran of the sea."

Osmund blushed and said nothing. But his smile showed how pleased he was by his father's compliment.

During the last part of the story, no one had noticed that Arnulf had disappeared. But all at once the back door was thrown open and he came in, carrying two pigeons whose feathers were so drenched that he left a wet trail behind him.

"They were in Pan's doghouse," Arnulf said breathlessly. "And all the others are out there too. Can I take them in and dry them by the kitchen stove?"

"Suppose they fly on top of the stove, what then?" Astrid asked.

At that moment Sven put in his appearance, as dripping wet as the pigeons. Solveig had a sudden feeling of guilt, for it had not once occurred to her to wonder about Sven during the storm.

"I worried about you," Mrs. Nordland said. "But of course it was impossible to look for you."

"I was in the potato patch, digging up potatoes," Sven said. "The storm came up so sudden that I didn't realize anything was happening until it got pitch dark. I thought of the storm cellar. It is close by, you know. But then I remembered how lightning often strikes trees and Lily would get under a good big one out in the pasture. So I ran as fast as I could, and sure enough, she was under the biggest of them all. She didn't want to come along, and I had to pull and tug to get her into the barn. And when we both finally left the barn, I saw that the lightning had struck that very tree and two others."

"Thank you, Sven," Mrs. Nordland said quietly. "We are deeply grateful."

"Mamma, can I dry my pigeons by the kitchen fire?" Arnulf demanded, still holding the wet birds.

"They might start flying around and get singed by the stove," Solveig objected.

"I'll get a big box for them," Sven said, "and cover it with that extra screen we have out in the shed."

While supper was being assembled, Mr. Nordland and Sven went out to look over the damage. Arnulf's pigeon house had been blown off the roof of the shed. Nearly every tree except the evergreens had broken branches, and the fruit was lying on the ground in mounds. But the windmill was safe, and there was not much damage in the vineyard.

The most amazing result of the storm was the absolute destruction of the storm cellar.

"It's certainly a good thing no one went there," Mr. Nordland said when they were back at the house and having supper. What must have happened, he explained, was that the tall oak at the top of the hill was blown down or struck by lightning, and it came crashing against the trap door in the hillside which led into the storm cellar. Then the torrential rain must have flooded the place and caused a small landslide.

"We were all fortunate to escape with our lives," Mrs. Nordland said. "Including Arnulf's pigeons."

"And to think only Pan knew the storm was coming up," Solveig said. "Don't you remember, Mamma, how he came in and lay whining under the ironing board?"

"Nature has a way of protecting animals," Mrs. Nordland said.

"But if Lily had stayed under the tree," Astrid said,

"she would have been killed. It was Sven that took care of her."

"You think you're so smart," Arnulf scoffed.

"Hush, children," his mother said. "Haven't you noticed what a beautiful evening God is sending us now? We've never had sweeter smelling air. We must be thankful for everything, and we must not be forgetful of telling Him so."

CHAPTER NINE

SOLVEIG looked at her reflection in the mirror. Her royal blue silk tie matched the blue ribbon around her head, and the bows of each were as right as she could make them. They helped at least a little to offset the plainness of her white sailor suit. She would have liked to have worn her silk mull dress or her orchid-colored organdy, but her mother had dissuaded her.

"After all, it isn't as if the Worthingtons had invited you to a party," she had told Solveig.

"But, Mamma, the people at the hotel dress elegantly all the time," Solveig had objected.

"They are rich people from the South. You are a schoolgirl living modestly in your summer home. I'm sure you will feel comfortable in your sailor suit."

Solveig's white shoes were almost new, and so were the cotton stockings which she had just put on. When she came downstairs, her mother gave her a smile of approval.

"You look very pretty, dear," she told Solveig.

For once Osmund had made no objection to dressing up. When he came out on the porch wearing his new blue serge suit, his stiff high collar, and blue and white tie, Solveig thought he was absolutely handsome and was proud to be accompanying him to the hotel. She complimented him on his appearance, and he bowed and said, "Out of respect and loyalty and deference to my dear sister."

The twins stood beside their mother and waved to Solveig and Osmund as they started down for the lake shore. And little Helga, in her mother's arms, waved a gay farewell too.

"Be careful," Mrs. Nordland called after them.

The water down by the dock was covered with a thick green scum, and to the right yellow and white water lilies bloomed.

"Do you remember," Solveig said to Osmund, "how Mrs. Hegstrom up in the country told Papa that in August everything bloomed and even the water bloomed too? Only in her Swedish it sounded even more romantic."

Osmund had unfastened the boat and was seated at the oars. "Mrs. Hegstrom never struck me as being particularly romantic," he said, "running around her farm in an old calico dress."

"Now you're forgetting your own standard philosophy," Solveig teased him from the back seat. "You know how you and Arnulf always object to being dressed up."

Osmund started to row vigorously, sending the boat spinning and leaving the bow pointed in the direction of the station. The farther they got out on the lake the clearer the water grew. A fresh breeze blew up, just enough to send tiny waves lapping against the boat.

"I think it was awfully nice of Morton and Patricia to invite us." Solveig beamed.

"I hope the hotel has good cooks," Osmund said. "I'm hungry already."

"You act as though you didn't put away a perfectly enormous breakfast this morning," said Solveig. "I hope——"

"Now don't start preaching," Osmund said. "We're out to enjoy ourselves today."

Walking up the boardwalk to the hotel as a guest gave Solveig an entirely different feeling than when she went to ask for the mail. This time she had a sense of really belonging, and that was very pleasant. Today the rows and rows of windows at the top in the brown peaked gables impressed her more than ever. In fact, everything about this hotel was perfect.

Why couldn't her father, who was an architect and understood perfection, have acquired more of it at their place on Saga Hill? Granted that the nasturtiums growing on their ash pile were larger and more luxuriant than those along the fence of the hotel, but they were simply a mass of bright flowers, with no order in the flower bed at all.

Morton and Patricia were waiting for them on the veranda. At least, that was what the people at the hotel called it. At home there were only porches.

"We began to worry for fear something might have upset your plans," said Patricia. At once Solveig was relieved to see that she was wearing a dress almost as plain as her own. "Especially after yesterday's storm."

"As a matter of fact," said Osmund, "I thought for a

while last evening that there would be no party for me. My father and I came out from town last night and got caught in it."

"You don't mean to say you were out in a boat?" said Morton with real concern in his voice.

"We were in Deering's steamer, and if the old Cap hadn't been such a fine seaman, I'm afraid the show might have had a pretty sad ending."

I hope he doesn't go into detail, thought Solveig, and explain why he happened to be in town. Morton wore his spotless white suit so casually that she didn't want Osmund to start explaining what an effort the family had gone to to procure his blue serge.

"Well, we're certainly grateful to Captain Deering for bringing you and your father safely to land," Morton said. Then, taking Solveig's arm, he continued, "They're already beginning to serve in the dining room. And if you people are half as hungry as I am, you're ready to eat."

Solveig had never been in the hotel dining room, and as far as she knew Osmund hadn't either. Although with boys you never could tell. Osmund was younger than she was, but he seemed to get around much more.

It was pleasantly cool in the large, spacious room with many small tables, and Solveig felt as though she were moving in a fairy tale, being escorted by such a handsome young man. A gentleman dressed in black came toward them.

"I saved the table by the window just as you asked me to," he said.

Morton held her chair until she sank into it. Then she looked anxiously across the table and held her breath until she saw Osmund do the same for Patricia. Osmund was continuing to be loyal to her.

There was nothing very special about the food: chicken croquettes, a salad, small rolls, and coffee. Her mother gave them more and better food at home. But to have a waitress, smartly dressed in black with a white cap and apron, anticipate your every want, even to pouring water for you, struck Solveig as the height of high living. And she was awed by the assurance with which Morton ordered more butter and an alternate dessert which was not on the menu.

When the finger bowls arrived Solveig was baffled and waited until Morton dipped his fingers in his so that she could follow his example. When she cast a glance in Osmund's direction he was already drying his fingers on his napkin, and she made up her mind then and there to stop worrying about him. He was getting along much better than she was and was perfectly at ease, and Solveig suddenly felt a new pride in her younger brother.

By the time the four young people returned to the veranda, a number of people were seated there watching the boats on the Upper Lake. This was a much larger body of water than West Arm and was dotted with boats of every size and variety.

"I'd like you to meet some friends of my parents," Morton said, moving toward a distinguished-looking couple who were sitting a short distance away. "Mr. and Mrs. Franklin have just returned from Paris and brought greetings to us from our father and mother."

Paris! And how nonchalantly Morton mentioned his parents' being there. If she were doing the introducing she would have to say, "My father is at his office in town, and my mother is home taking care of the twins and our baby."

After exchanging a few words with this couple and with

a few other equally distinguished and far-traveled people, Morton said, "Patricia and I thought we might take you for a sail. This year we're renting a boat for the season. Would you like to?"

For a moment Solveig hesitated. There were three things which her father had forbidden the family to have at the lake. One was a gasoline stove, although her mother had wanted one for years, since cooking on a kerosene stove and a wood range was not nearly as satisfactory in the summer time. The two other things were a canoe and a sailboat, either of which she and Osmund would have liked to have. But her father had always turned a deaf ear to their suggestions. "There are already too many things with which you children could destroy yourselves, if you set out to do it," he always said.

But, after all, they would not be owning this boat. Morton and Patricia would be in charge. "We'd love to, wouldn't we, Osmund?" she said, her heart skipping a beat.

Osmund said nothing. But after they had stepped into the boat, Solveig was surprised to find that he knew almost as much about sailing as the two Worthingtons did.

"I suppose you'll want to manage the sheets for the mainsail and the tiller," he told Morton. "Would you like me to help Patricia with the sheets for the jib?" He made way for Patricia to the back of the boat and then sat down beside her.

Solveig felt both proud and resentful. She was proud that a member of the family knew enough about sailing so that the Worthingtons would not feel the Nordlands grew up in the sticks, but at the same time she felt left out and inferior. After Helga grew a little bigger and did not require so much care, and when the twins got more sense and were not so prone to mischief, she was going to make a terrific effort to get out more and learn about the world.

But at that very moment Morton said, "It's a good thing, Osmund, you didn't try to appropriate that sister of yours too. She and I are going to do the steering."

Then he tactfully showed her where to sit, and Solveig could have wept in gratitude for his kindness. After that she watched his every movement and followed his instructions to the letter. It was her first experience in a sailboat, and she meant to learn as much as she could from it.

When Morton gave Osmund the order to tack, the boat started zigzagging over the water. When it made a sharp turn and tipped so far to one side that the sails almost touched the water, he called out, "To port and lean over the gunwale," at the same time taking Solveig firmly by the arm and pulling her to the opposite side of the boat. They all four leaned over the edge of the boat as far as they could, and slowly but surely it righted itself.

For a while after that the wind seemed to be just right and they glided over the water much as Solveig had seen other sailboats do as she watched from the shore. This gave her an opportunity to talk to Morton, and she explained that although she had lived at the lake every summer of her life she knew absolutely nothing about sailing. "But Papa only said we couldn't own a sailboat," she finished. "I never heard him say we couldn't go into one."

Morton threw his head back and laughed. "I had better see to it that I bring you back to shore safely, so your father doesn't add that amendment to his law." Then his face sobered. "But I can see your father's point of view.

There are a lot of drownings that come from taking too
many chances."

When they were finally back on land, Morton suggested,
"What would you people say to some ice cream down at
the casino? I've worked up an appetite out on the water."

Solveig had not thought to bring a penny along, and
as far as she knew Osmund didn't have any money either.
Actual cash money was very scarce at their home, unless
it was given out for some special thing that was to be pur-
chased. But to come right out and say this would have
been impossibly humiliating, so she went along with the
others down to the casino.

"Let's sit out on the veranda above the water," Patricia
said. The tables close to the railing permitted the four to
be almost as close to the water as they had been in the
sailboat.

For a moment Solveig was miserable. Then Morton
said, "If you people don't mind, I'm ordering a banana
dream for each of us." And when the waiter came along
he told him to give him the check so he could sign it
and have it put on his bill.

Solveig breathed easier. Now she could really enjoy
the treat. And what a treat it was: a foundation of vanilla
ice cream and a layer of bananas and chopped nuts and a
mixture of other fruits, all smothered in whipped cream.
These layers were repeated twice and on top of all was a
candied cherry. Except for the mixed fruits, which Solveig
did not recognize, her mother could have furnished the
other ingredients at home. But who would dream up such
concoctions and have the patience to put them together?

Sitting on the veranda over the lake, with two such
romantic young people as Patricia and Morton Worthington, and being waited on by a white-clad young man from

the ice-cream counter—it was too heavenly to be described.

"Didn't you say you were taking us bowling?" Patricia asked.

Morton smiled indulgently. "Give me time," he said. "Solveig hasn't finished her banana dream yet."

When she had finished and the four were in the bowling alley, Solveig did not worry about her lack of money. There seemed to be no end to the Worthington resources, and she might as well enjoy every minute of this miraculous day while she had the chance.

As far as the game itself was concerned, her part in it was almost a complete failure. Invariably the ball rolled to the side and the pins were left standing untouched.

"You bowl just like Patricia," Morton said.

Solveig felt her cheeks grow hot. How could she tell him that this was the first time she had ever held a ball in a bowling alley?

"We concentrate on croquet," said Osmund, and Solveig could have kissed him for coming to her defense. "You should see the way she can shoot croquet balls at home."

In spite of Osmund's reason for her bad bowling, he did very well himself. And when the scores were added up, his and Patricia's team came out almost as well as hers and Morton's.

"There's a tennis match over at the hotel grounds," Patricia said. "Would you like to watch the players for a little while?"

"It must be almost over," Morton said. "But we might go and see."

It was interesting for Solveig, who had never seen a tennis match, to watch the agile players send the ball over the net. But, as Morton had said, the game was almost over, and Solveig was sorry to have it end so soon.

"I wonder what time it's getting to be?" she asked.

Morton pulled a gold watch from his pocket. "Just half-past five," he said.

"Then I'm afraid we'll have to get started for home," Solveig said reluctantly.

But, as they were going down the boardwalk toward the station, strains of music came from the direction of the picnic grounds.

"Oh," Morton exclaimed, "I forgot all about the outing the pharmacists are having today. Mr. Seldon said there would be dancing and they were having a fine orchestra."

"Neither Osmund nor I dance," Solveig said.

"Wouldn't you like to listen to the music anyway?"

Solveig hesitated.

"Oh, come on," Osmund said. "If I row real hard we won't be late getting home."

The music was beautiful—a piano, a violin, and a clarinet—and the place was crowded with dancers. Suddenly the orchestra struck up the "Blue Danube Waltz," and Solveig began to tap one foot in time to the music.

"I knew you had rhythm," Morton declared. "I could tell it from the way you walk. Don't you want to try this dance with me?"

Solveig shook her head. "Thank you for asking me, but I just couldn't." She had managed to come out of the sailing experience fairly well, and she couldn't risk spoiling things by floundering around and making a spectacle of herself.

Morton made a little bow. "When you do start dancing, Solveig, I shall consider it a privilege to be one of your first partners."

Solveig's cheeks burned even hotter. Who but a true

southern gentleman could speak so beautifully and with such genuine feeling?

Morton and Patricia walked down to the boat with them. "It was sure a lot of fun," Osmund said.

"We loved having you," said Patricia.

"Mamma would like you both to spend a Sunday with us," Solveig said suddenly.

"You won't have to ask us twice," Morton said.

"We'll let you know the date," said Solveig. "It depends on when my father is home. And thank you for a wonderful afternoon."

Osmund took long, deep strokes with the oars, and they were home in record time.

"How did you enjoy your outing?" Mrs. Nordland asked.

"It was swell," Osmund said.

"And you, Solveig?"

"The Worthingtons are the most wonderful people in the whole world."

"When your father comes out tomorrow we will talk things over and decide which Sunday will be the best for him. And then you, Osmund, can invite them at the same time you call for the mail at the hotel."

"But, Mamma," said Solveig, "we will have to plan something for them to do when they are here. You should have seen all the things they thought of to entertain us. And here there's just nothing."

Mrs. Nordland smiled. "I wouldn't worry too much about that if I were you. If they are the kind of young people I take them for, they will fit right in with the family and we'll get along all right."

"I'll let them play croquet with me," Astrid piped up. "And I bet I beat them too."

"Bragger," said Arnulf. "Anyhow, they probably don't play croquet."

"They can sit in our swing and we'll play train," Astrid suggested.

"I'll let them come with me when I dig angleworms," Arnulf said. "There's a swell place behind the shed for grubworms too."

"Honestly, Mamma," said Solveig, much upset. "Please make the twins behave when the Worthingtons come. And as for you, Osmund——"

"If I may offer a humble suggestion," said Osmund, "let Mamma give them some of her good cooking. It will make the hotel chefs seem like amateurs."

"It isn't polite to criticize the food when you're a guest," Solveig said. "And anyway, they can't eat all the time they're here."

"It's my favorite form of entertainment," Osmund said. "And I'll bet it's Morton's too."

"There will be plenty of good food for our guests," Mrs. Nordland said soothingly. "And there is no need for you to worry about the behavior of the family, Solveig. I'm sure the young people will be more than pleased to spend a day with us just doing what we naturally do on Sundays. Of course, if you or Osmund can think of anything special they might enjoy, there is no reason for your not suggesting it to them. And now I think there has been enough discussion of the subject."

But Solveig still felt dubious, and all evening she kept trying to think of some wonderful way in which she could entertain the Worthingtons. It made her feel a little resentful of the narrow environment in which her parents had kept her. She knew nothing about sailing or bowling or tennis or dancing. Neither she nor Osmund ever had any cash unless it was something their parents had especially planned for them. They never traveled anywhere except between Minneapolis and their lake home. And their father's chief ambition for them seemed to be that they should be practically perfect in all the subjects they studied in school, stand up straight, and walk with the kind of military bearing he had acquired during his training in the Norwegian army.

Yet in spite of everything, Solveig looked forward to the Sunday when Morton and Patricia would be entertained, even in a limited way, in their home. And she could only hope that things wouldn't seem too boring to them.

CHAPTER TEN

IT WAS Sunday morning, the special Sunday morning when the Worthingtons were coming to spend the day. They would board Deering's steamer when the captain met the ten-o'clock morning train and would land at their dock about half an hour later.

Solveig was the first of the family to come downstairs, and she had already been awake a long time. If breakfast could be pushed ahead, and the dishes washed, and the kitchen cleared, and the house gone over for the last time, and fresh flowers picked and placed attractively in the parlor and the dining room, and the dinner gotten well under way, at least some of the usual Sunday confusion might be avoided. And there would be time to get little Helga and the twins dressed at the last minute so that they would present a creditable appearance to begin with anyway. And in case the twins should get too messy before the day was over, Solveig had prevailed upon her mother to have an extra outfit ready for each of them.

Saturday had been more than hectic. There had been, of course, a great deal of actual work to be done. And for once in her life Solveig had had heated arguments with her mother.

The first occurred when the matter of clothes for Sunday came up. Solveig wanted her mother to wear one of her best summer dresses in order to make a good impression on the Worthingtons. To her surprise her mother had stood firm. She was going to wear one of her new house dresses with stiff cuffs and white starched collar. "There will be much to do," she said, "and I am not comfortable in anything else."

As for herself, Solveig had pictured herself all decked out in her pink dotted swiss, and her mother had given a flat no to this plan. A white skirt and one of her dainty voile blouses would be fully as becoming and much more appropriate. People in lake cottages did not put on frilly party dresses, especially when they had to help in the kitchen.

When it came to the matter of food, Solveig had to admit that her mother knew more about it than she did. The food served at the hotel had really not been as good as the meals her mother prepared at home. It was a question of how to serve the food on which they disagreed. Solveig wanted both meals served in the dining room, which would be elaborately decorated with flowers for the occasion, and she wanted the food itself brought in on plates all ready to be eaten. She thought it would be nice to set an extra small table for the twins, so they could not cause any disturbance during the meal. In the hotel dining room there had been many separate tables.

Her mother vetoed all these suggestions with unusual firmness. "It will be hot and stuffy in the dining room," she said. "The back porch will be much more comfortable. We'll have dinner at twelve sharp, as your father likes it, and that will give us a long afternoon. He brought out a beautiful pork roast last night and he'll carve this at the table, and I will serve the mashed potatoes and gravy. The carrots and peas can be passed around, and so can the sliced tomatoes and the lettuce. We'll serve this with vinegar and sugar just as your father likes it."

"But the twins——"

"They will be much more apt to behave if things are done in the usual way," her mother told her. "Besides, this is their home and we have to put up with them. We'll serve coffee and a cream cake out in the arbor in the middle of the afternoon and a picnic supper out on the lawn. There will be cold meat, potato salad, rolls, and buttered bread."

"And for dessert?" Solveig asked, now thoroughly subdued.

"For dinner at this time of year I would like to give your father apple pie from his own trees and homemade ice cream. If there is any pie left, and there is always plenty of ice cream, I'm sure those young people won't object to the same thing for supper too."

Now that the actual day of the Worthingtons' arrival had come, Solveig was filled with mixed emotions. Suppose her father monopolized their attention for the greater part of the day? He might insist on showing them his apple trees in the heat of midday, or have them trudge over to his grape arbor while he expounded all the varieties he had planted there.

If only he would smoke cigars instead of puffing at his

old pipe. Or wear his dignified business suit instead of the plaid jacket and the trousers that were goodness knows how old. Even her mother had tried to get him to dress differently at the lake, but in that matter she could not move him. He loved to put on these clothes, take his pipe, turn on the water hydrant, go into the apple orchard, and give every tree there a soaking on Sunday morning. He did this whether there had been plenty of rain or not, and during this last week there had been no rain.

The twins were always unpredictable. And although there wasn't a sweeter little girl than Helga and she had been trained to the best of bathroom habits, she might get excited and have an accident. And if Patricia or Morton were holding her when the unexpected happened, Solveig knew she would never get over the unfortunate incident. As for Osmund, she hoped he would be on his best behavior, but one could never depend on it.

But she could always trust her mother to do the right thing, even though she might not always agree with her. And after all, the Worthingtons were really coming and it should be one of the happiest days of her life.

Solveig put the coffee on the stove to boil, fried the ham and eggs, and set the table, so that when the family came downstairs for breakfast everything was ready for them.

"Ellen, we did right in ordering a daughter for our oldest child," her father said, taking his place at the head of the table. "Pretty soon you'll have nothing to do but sit in the parlor like a lady."

"I always knew I was the lucky one," said Osmund.

"There is wood to be carried into the house," his mother reminded him. "And there is also the ice cream to be frozen."

The entire family was in high spirits, and the morning went quietly until there came three sharp whistles from Captain Deering's steamer. The pointed bow of the red steamer was making its way to their dock.

Impatient as Solveig had been all morning, she was now seized with a sudden shyness, almost a panic. As the family went down the hill she lagged behind, and as the steamer docked she stood some distance away.

The two Worthingtons were dressed almost alike in white sailor suits, and for the first time Solveig was struck by their remarkable resemblance to each other. Patricia was slighter and her features were more delicate, but it would have been clear to anyone that they were brother and sister.

Solveig watched her father and Osmund shake hands with them. She could not hear what was being said, but they were all smiling. Then her mother went forward, carrying Helga, and greeted them also.

At that instant the twins took over, Arnulf hugging Morton's arm and Astrid Patricia's. Solveig could not help wondering what their probably grimy hands were doing to the clean sleeves, but the Worthingtons did not seem to notice, and immediately the twins were each clasping what looked like a large box of candy.

Solveig could delay her greeting no longer. As if the twins had given each other a secret signal they tore open their boxes, plunked some chocolate into their mouths, and started up the hill on a run. And for once Solveig was grateful for their greediness.

"Such a beautiful place," said Morton, as they shook hands. "I never saw such evergreens in my life."

"We loved seeing your flag," said Patricia. "Captain Deering said that you raise it every Sunday."

"I grew up with the custom in Norway," Mr. Nordland said. "In addition to being a mark of respect to our country, the flag was a sort of symbol of welcome to any guests that might come during the day. There was a great deal of work to be done on our farm in Norway, since we were ten children and there were many mouths to feed, and so Sunday was really the visiting day for everyone."

Solveig was both proud and embarrassed at what her father had said. It was a beautiful speech, to be sure. But why did he, and her mother, too, for that matter, always keep reminding people that they came from large families and had been born and brought up in Norway?

"I think that's wonderful," Morton said. "And so we feel doubly welcome here today."

It seemed no time at all before dinner was ready to be served. As soon as everyone was seated at the porch table the twins, in unison, started to say the blessing in Norwegian, just as they usually did. Solveig had learned it in English and had planned to say it herself, but as usual the twins were too quick for her.

After grace had been said, Solveig brought in the hot food from the kitchen and then sat down beside Arnulf. Morton was at the far end of the table on the same side so that she could not see his face, and she hoped that Astrid, who was sitting beside him, would not try to show off. Then she looked across the table, and it suddenly came to her that the Worthingtons would certainly think it was queer to have the hired man eating with them. She had not given this a thought before, since Sven seemed almost a part of the family. But as she sat facing him Solveig was filled with misgivings. His sandy hair was much too long and plastered down to his head by an overapplication of water. Why hadn't she seen to it that he got a haircut?

And he was obviously uncomfortable in his navy serge suit, which was much too big for him.

"Such beautiful lettuce and tomatoes," Patricia said, helping herself generously.

Solveig felt a little easier. These Worthingtons at least weren't too proper to praise the food on the table. Somewhere she had read in a book of etiquette that one should never make remarks about the food that was being served, but Patricia evidently did not agree with the book.

"Sven is our gardener," Mr. Nordland said. "He grows all our fruits and vegetables."

"I wish the Hotel Del Otero could get him," said Morton. "We haven't had anything like this all summer."

And then, to Solveig's surprise, Sven began to explain how he went about raising small vegetables. He preferred to start with seeds, he said, and transplant the tender shoots into larger containers. And he made several trips out to the lake in the early spring to get the plants in the ground at exactly the right time. Morton interrupted him several times to ask questions. Then the subject changed to fishing and sailing, and the upshot was that Morton asked Sven to come and teach him some of the pointers which all Norwegian sailors took for granted.

Morton had two pieces of pie and both of them were heaped with ice cream. And the twins had been so busy stuffing themselves that they had behaved remarkably well. Solveig breathed a sigh of relief, and at that moment little Helga raised both her milk glass and the tray of her high chair together and her end of the table was deluged.

"We usually count on at least one accident during each meal," said her mother easily, using her napkin for the preliminary mopping up. "When the older children were Helga's age there were many more."

How could her mother take things so placidly? Solveig wondered. Or why did she herself have to be so perturbed about everything?

After dinner Mr. Nordland said, "How would you young people like to see our apple orchard and our vineyard?"

Solveig's heart sank. What possible interest could grapes and apples have for young people from an elegant city like St. Louis, except to eat them? Well, there was no help for it. Perhaps she could go along and distract their attention once in a while so that the tour of inspection wouldn't become too boring.

"This is my best apple tree," her father said as they reached the orchard. "It's a Whitney crab, and its fruit is as sweet as sugar. Since it was little more than a seedling it has never failed to bear a good crop. This year it had such a heavy load we had to prop the branches up to keep them from breaking."

He picked up a rosy apple and handed it to Morton.

"Mmm," said Morton, chewing his first bite. "I could eat these by the dozen."

"That's what the children do," Mr. Nordland said, "and it never seems to hurt them any." He took several puffs from his pipe, as he always did when he was really pleased. "Now these Dutchess apples are primarily for eating. They are the first to ripen, and we eat most of them before we move back to the city." He picked a large red one, and Morton, who had finished his Whitney crab, started munching on it.

"Papa, if you fill Morton up with apples he won't be able to enjoy his supper," Solveig protested.

Morton chuckled. "You don't know me. My mother says there is no bottom to my stomach."

"You wouldn't enjoy these Okabenas," Mr. Nordland said. "They ripen later. And we seldom eat many Wealthies before late fall. We wrap them separately in tissue paper and preserve them in boxes, a bushel at a time, and they keep until well after Christmas. They can even be eaten as late as March if they are kept cool in the vegetable cellar."

"Those large green ones, what are they?" Morton asked.

"They are Patent Greenings. They're not much for eating, but Mrs. Nordland will bake pies with them all fall."

"Boy, I'd love to take a book and spend all day in this apple orchard," Morton said, and from the tone of his voice Solveig knew that he wasn't being bored.

When they arrived at the vineyard, which was on a sunny hillside sloping to the south, Patricia and Osmund joined them.

"Morton, you should see those seven-year-old twins play croquet," his sister said. "They beat Osmund and me to smithereens."

But Morton was not interested in his sister's croquet score. He was sampling a bunch of grapes and listening with marked attention to what Mr. Nordland was saying to him.

"Grapes are much more difficult to raise than apples. You plant an apple tree, make sure it gets plenty of water, spray it for insects, and wrap the trunk in burlap in the fall to protect it from rabbits. But grape vines have to be covered with earth and hay every fall and fastened up again in the spring. And it is necessary to cultivate between the rows to keep the weeds from smothering them and to see the wires are stretched properly so that the vines are held up and that the posts are standing straight."

Then he pointed out the different varieties of grapes— the small red Delawares, the dark blue Concords, the purple Rogers and New Brightons, and the dainty green Lady grapes. Morton asked questions, and Mr. Nordland carefully explained the answers to them all.

"I'm gradually being converted into becoming a fruit farmer at Lake Minnetonka," Morton said to Solveig. "It must be fascinating to live here."

"It's a pleasant hobby," Mr. Nordland said. "I only wish I could stay out here more and enjoy it. But it's good for the family to be here during the summer."

"You never told me about this marvelous place," Morton said to Solveig. "If it were mine I'd be boasting about it from the housetops."

Back at the house they were greeted by Mrs. Nordland. "The coffee is boiled and the cream is whipped, ready to put on the cake, and the table is set out in the grape arbor."

"Who ever heard of such a life?" Morton exclaimed. "How do you suppose we are going to stand it back at the hotel, Patricia?"

Solveig was even more impressed by Morton's good manners. How nice of him to speak of his visit in such terms, when he was living at a hotel that was perfection itself.

But she had to admit that it was cool and pleasant in the grape arbor. The deep green leaves were, even in the late summer, so luxuriant that they formed an almost impenetrable ceiling and walls to shut out the hot afternoon sun. The twins and Patricia preferred root beer, cold and refreshing from the icehouse, with the cream cake.

The others, in spite of the heat, enjoyed the steaming coffee.

As Morton was being helped to his last piece of cake, Astrid asked, "Mamma, can Morton and Patricia play croquet with Arnulf and me?"

"Yup, and we'll beat them," Arnulf put in with enthusiasm.

"Mamma," Solveig began pleadingly, "don't let them ——"

The piece of cake was a small one, and as he swallowed the last mouthful Morton said, "I'll take you on. Come on, Patricia."

The four of them went off together, and Solveig turned to her mother. "Mamma, why didn't you make the twins stop bothering them?"

"Because Morton and Patricia will enjoy the game and it will give you and me a chance to get all the supper things ready."

It was wonderful the way her mother was always able to figure things out. The kitchen was small, and it would have been crowded if more than two had tried to work in it. And it was fun preparing the potato salad and slicing the ham and getting all the other food ready. All was set out on the kitchen table ready to be carried out on the lawn when Astrid came charging into the kitchen.

"We beat them," she shouted. "Every game we beat them."

"They are wonderful at croquet," said Morton, following her in. "They should be real athletes some day."

There was enthusiasm in his voice, and Solveig knew he was not merely being polite. She herself had always considered their addiction to croquet a convenient way of escaping the small duties their mother expected them to perform.

It was while they were eating their supper on the lawn that Morton suddenly said, "Mr. Nordland, I have a confession to make."

Everyone looked startled and Solveig felt uneasy.

"The other day when Osmund and Solveig were visiting us, I took them sailing. I didn't realize that you objected to sailing, and it was only after we were already out on the lake that I learned how you felt about it."

"I told him you only objected to owning a boat," said Solveig. "You didn't say anything about sailing with other people."

Mr. Nordland smiled. "You have me there, Solveig," he said. "And I guess I won't have to worry when you're out with as responsible a young man as Morton."

Solveig could not help but feel relieved. It had bothered her ever since her visit to the Worthingtons that she had deceived her father, in spirit if not according to the letter, and it pleased her, too, that Morton had been honest about the sailing even if it meant her father's possible disapproval.

The sun had almost reached the horizon when Mr. Nordland said it was time to let down the flag, and he let Morton handle the ropes.

"Why, it's exactly like tacking when you're out sailing," he said.

"It's the same principle," Mr. Nordland agreed.

"Did you ever go sailing?" Solveig asked her father.

"When I was in Norway as a boy, yes. Along the fjords. And I've had some very narrow escapes. That is why I have been so reluctant to allow you children to do it."

Astrid insisted on taking Patricia upstairs to brush up

before leaving, and Solveig and Morton strolled out on the lawn.

"It's been a perfect day," Morton told her. "I never knew people could live as your family does."

Solveig looked at him in surprise.

"My sister and I scarcely know what family life is. Our parents travel a great deal and we seldom see them. During the winter we're off at school, and in the summer we're usually sent to some resort."

"But living at the Hotel Del Otero—that must be wonderful," Solveig said.

"Well, this summer has been less boring than most. Really not half bad, partly because we've come to know you and Osmund. As for today, and your parents—Solveig, you and your brothers and sisters should count yourselves the most fortunate people on earth. With such a father and mother and such a home——"

Solveig was too surprised to speak.

"It's hard for me not to feel envious. But do you know, I am going to try and get my father to let me come north and attend your University of Minnesota this fall. I'm starting a pre-med course, and my uncle, who is a doctor, says that it's one of the best schools in the country."

"If you do come," said Solveig, trying her best to keep the eagerness out of her voice, "I know my parents would welcome you to our home in Minneapolis. That is, if you would care to come."

"Just try to keep me away," Morton said.

"I'm ready to leave now," said Patricia from the front porch.

"I'm not," said Morton in a low voice as he held Solveig's hand. Together they walked slowly back to the house where the family was waiting to say good-bye and to wish them Godspeed.

After they had left Mrs. Nordland went upstairs to put Helga and the twins to bed. Osmund and her father went with Sven to check on a break in the pasture fence, and Solveig was left to wash the dishes.

After the kitchen had been tidied up, Solveig went out on the front porch and sat down in the hammock. Evening was coming on, and down at the Sathers' there was a soft glow from their rose-colored globe lamp. Edith was close to the table, probably reading the week's installment of the novel from their Norwegian paper to her parents, as she always did on Sunday nights.

There was a smoky haziness in the air, so that the distant shore line no longer marked the place where the sky ended and the lake began. The feel of the air reminded Solveig that autumn was almost here, and a sudden sadness came over her. All day, during the visit of the Worthingtons, summer seemed still at its height, but now Solveig realized that the season was nearly over.

She remembered that in the spring she had almost disliked the prospect of spending the summer at Lake Minnetonka. How she had envied the other girls of her age who were going visiting or taking jobs or doing anything more exciting than vegetating out at their own cottage at the lake. In fact, it seemed to Solveig that she had spent a lot of her time envying other people, and she couldn't remember why.

She yawned comfortably and settled herself lower in the hammock. If Morton's father permitted him to attend the University of Minnesota next winter, she was sure that her parents would invite him often to their home. They had cozy times in Minneapolis, too, sitting around the fireplace, eating Sunday-night suppers, celebrating Thanks-givings with a huge turkey dinner, a goose at Christmas, and all their birthdays with cakes and presents.

And perhaps next summer she might manage things so that he would be invited to spend some of his vacation at their cottage instead of in a big, lonely hotel.